IN TOO DEEP

Also by Dwayne S. Joseph

Choices Men Make
Womanizers
Never Say Never
If Your Girl Only Knew

Anthologies:
Around the Way Girls
Gigolos Get Lonely Too

IN TOO DEEP

DWAYNE S. JOSEPH

URBAN Renaissance
www.urbanbooks.net

Urban Books, LLC
78 East Industry Court
Deer Park, NY 11729

In Too Deep Copyright © 2007 Dwayne S. Joseph

All rights reserved. No part of this book may be repro-
duced in any form or by any means without prior con-
sent of the Publisher, excepting brief quotes used in
reviews.

ISBN-13: 978-1-60162-225-9
ISBN-10: 1-60162-225-2

First Trade Paperback Printing September 2007
First Mass Paperback Printing August 2010
Printed in the United States of America

10 9 8 7 6 5 4 3 2 1

Distributed by Kensington Publishing Corp.
Submit Wholesale Orders to:
Kensington Publishing Corp.
C/O Penguin Group (USA) Inc.
Attention: Order Processing
405 Murray Hill Parkway
East Rutherford, NJ 07073-2316
Phone: 1-800-526-0275
Fax: 1-800-227-9604

Acknowledgments

God: Thank you for EVERYTHING.

To Wendy, Tati, and Nati: I love you!

To Mom, Dad, Daren, Teyana, Evan, Granny, Grandmother, and the rest of my family: Love you all! Pat, Mike, Christina: it hasn't been easy, but we're surviving. Kirt: still and always will be in your corner, kid.

To my friends: Too many to name, but you know who you are. My Friday night Xbox 360 crew: Chris, Scott, Gregg, Russ, Jay, Shawn, Steve: is there a better guys' hangout! Bring your A game!

To Carl, Martha, Arvita, Roy, and the rest of the Urban Books team: Thanks for caring about our careers. To La Jill Hunt . . . who got your back, twin? Red . . . you're an Eagles fan, but I still got love for you. Eric Pete: Can't stop. Won't stop. Believe that. Now hurry and come on over the 360 side of the force! Robilyn Heath: You know you're still the Mother Hen. Portia Cannon: BIG love for you! Thank you a million times.

To the peeps I've met through myspace.com . . . thanks for shouting out and letting me know you enjoy the books. Peron: man the time is coming.

To the book clubs: One Book @ A Time, the African Violets Book Club, The Sweet Soul Sisters Book Club, African American Sisters In Spirit Book Club, Sisters In Spirit II, Brown Sugar Sistahs With Books, Page Turnas Book Club, For Da Sista's Book Club, Aminia Book Club, Circle Of Sisters, Ujima Nia, Sister 2 Sister Book Club, Ebony Jewels Book Club, Sistah On The Reading Edge, Cushcity.com Book Club, Between the Covers Literary Group . . . I TRULY, TRULY enjoyed meeting with you all and I loved each and every lively discussion. Believe me, I am the one who is honored. I sincerely and anxiously look forward to meeting with you all again! For those that I haven't had a chance to visit YET . . . I thank you for choosing my books to read, and I look forward to meeting with you.

To the readers: My deepest thanks for supporting my work. Please keep the e-mails and reviews coming. I truly appreciate them. Missy "Misherald" Brown . . . much thanks!!

To my New York Giants: Tiki . . . all the fans miss you already. Eli . . . your time to shine. That Super Bowl is coming!!

Peace!

Dwayne S. Joseph
www.myspace.com/Dwaynesjoseph
Djoseph21044@yahoo.com

Randy

Damn.

Tina called my cell again. That made twenty times in three days. You would think that when I didn't answer or call back after the first ten calls, she would have gotten the hint and given up. But not her. She just wouldn't accept the fact that I was through with her. We'd been apart for more than three years, but she still swore that we were each other's soul mates, and insisted that no matter how much time passed, one day I'd come to my senses and realize she was the woman for me. Yeah right. Straight up, Tina was a nut job. I swear she has multiple personalities. Some days she could be really laid-back and pleasant to be around, and then other days she'd be the most conniving, crabby, self-centered bitch who'd have me wondering if she had permanent residence down in the underworld. If that wasn't enough, she could be so emotionally unstable sometimes that looking at her wrong would cause her to become depressed and as needy as a two-year-old.

If having a dual personality wasn't her problem, then I'd say being bipolar was. I'd actually made the mistake one day of saying that to her, and even worse, suggesting that maybe she see a doctor for a little help. Without even giving me a chance to explain where I had been coming from, Tina flew off the handle, literally spitting curse words in my face. Guess I should have expected that, considering the fact that she'd never really had the capacity to be rational.

Tina's a high-maintenance headache and a half. And with her modeling career having taken off, you couldn't say shit to her about anything. With her divinely blessed physique and beauty, Tina floated up into her own made-up stratosphere, high above the rest of us. Like Mr. T, I pitied the next fool that wound up being her man. Of course, that all depended on whether she'd leave me the hell alone. Had I been able to see past her sex appeal and damn near perfect pussy, I would have jumped ship before she had the chance to become tied to me forever.

I'd finally moved on and found peace and happiness with my fiancée, Monique, who I met a year after I'd finally officially broken things off with Tina. At that time, I wasn't looking to hook up with any other women; at least not for a relationship. After all of the shit I'd gone through with Tina, I just wanted to live unattached and drama free. But I guess since I wasn't out looking for love, love decided to look for me. I just wish it had found me before Tina had the chance to stop taking her birth control pills because they "caused cancer."

My daughter, Jalisa, had been born during the first of the two years I'd lasted with Tina. Now don't get me wrong, having Jalisa in my life is a blessing that I wouldn't trade for the world. I love my little princess and would give up my own life if it would save hers. I just wish that I could have had her with Monique. But as it is, Tina's my daughter's mother. Wish she wasn't, but that's just the way it is. Only because I wanted Jalisa to have as normal a life as she could going back and forth between parents, did I put up with Tina's shit as she stopped at nothing to consistently throw a monkey wrench into the life that Monique and I were trying to build together. Hence the blowing up of my cell and her attempts to get me back, such as the last time we'd spoken.

"How's my little girl doing?"

Nice and normal; that's how the call started out.

"She's fine."

Short and to the point, I wanted her to know that the last thing I wanted to do was be on the phone with her.

"Is she eating properly?"

"I haven't been reported for starving her yet."

"Is she doing her schoolwork?"

"Every night."

A sigh. "Tell her I miss her and can't wait to see her."

"Speaking of which, when are you going to be back? I thought the assignment was only supposed to last two weeks. You know you only have her for four months. You're losing one already, and there is no getting it back or getting extra time."

"We ran into a storm and the shoot was delayed for a week. We should be finished soon."

"How long does it take to snap a photo?"

"You know it's not that easy, Randall. Besides, I'm not the only model here. Of course, if you are that worried about my time with her, you could just hop on a plane and bring her here. The Bahamas are beautiful this time of the year, and it would give the three of us some good quality time together."

Quality time?

So began the transition of the conversation. Like a sucker, I took the bait.

"We don't need quality time, Tina. We're not a family."

"Randall, don't say that. We are a family. We should be together. That's how God planned it."

"Don't bring God into this. We're Jalisa's parents, and that's all."

"And why do you think He gave us Jalisa?"

I sighed but didn't respond, hoping that Tina would see that I wasn't interested in the answer. Of course my non-response meant nothing.

"He gave us that beautiful little girl to keep you and me together because He knows a good thing when He designs one."

"So now God is a designer?"

"Of course. He plans everything, and everything happens according to His plan. You and I met, fell in love, and had Jalisa. Planned. You're only delaying the inevitable by keeping us apart."

"Tina . . ."

"Randy, you and I are a natural fit. Why do you keep denying what you know is the truth."

"Tina . . ." I started again.

"Soul mates, Randy. Look it up. Our picture is there."

I clenched my jaws and squeezed my eyes shut tightly, knowing that if I didn't get off of the phone as soon as possible, I was going to get a migraine. "Tina, I have to get going, okay. I have plans."

Tina hmmph'd. "Plans with who? That yellow bitch?"

And so the migraine ensued. "All right," I said holding back the urge to toss my phone across the room, "conversation over. You want to call and talk about Jalisa, that's fine. But I told you the last time we talked that if you had any negative things to say about Monique, tell them to someone else. I don't have time for your fucking teenage bullshit."

"Randy, baby, I'm sorry. Don't hang up yet. Please. Don't be mad."

"Good–bye, Tina."

"Randy, wait. Please. Look, I'm sorry, okay. I know it was unnecessary and I was wrong for going there. It's just that . . . that . . ." Tina paused for a brief second and when she continued, she did so with tears. "I just love you so much. We fit together so well. Much more than you and that . . . that . . . We just belong together, and we should be together. It's what's right."

"I'm hanging up, Tina. Call me when you get back in the States and call before you come to pick

Jalisa up. I don't want Monique around when you come by."

"And why the hell not? Are you afraid that bitch will finally understand that she's outclassed and will leave you?"

Without a response, I ended the call. That was pretty much the pattern of our exchanges when-ever she called. We just used different words. It was damn frustrating. Jalisa was the only reason I made any effort at all to be civil with her, because I fig-ured the worst thing I could do was to let her see her mother and father going at it. My mother un-derstood my reasoning, but felt I was still being too nice, and insisted that if I didn't start putting my foot down, sooner or later Tina and her bullshit were going to damage my relationship with Mo-nique. Of course, that was the last thing I wanted to have happen.

From the first moment we met, we connected. I was in the mall struggling to find a stylish outfit for my mother's birthday. Shopping has never been one of my favorite things to do and after two hours of maybe and maybe nots, I was ready to call it quits and go with a gift certificate. That's when I bumped into Monique. Literally. I hadn't been paying attention to where I was going when we col-lided, and I caused her to drop a few of the bags she'd been holding. It took me a couple of sec-onds to react and apologize and help her pick up her things because when my eyes first settled on her, I found myself immediately captivated by a pair of feline light-brown eyes that were a cross somewhere between sensuality and mystery. As a matter of fact, I would have probably continued to stare at her, had she not cleared her throat.

I quickly said I was sorry a multitude of times and hurried to get her things. She smiled a beautiful smile with lips so perfect and full and held up her hand. "I'm fine, really," she'd said. She smiled again, and I could tell she was going to continue on with her own business, but I didn't want our meeting to end there. I extended my hand.

"I'm Randy."

"Monique," she said, slipping hers in mine.

"I apologize again. I don't make it a habit to not pay attention to where I'm going and bump into beautiful women."

She smiled that smile again. "No harm, no foul. Luckily for you I didn't have anything that was breakable," she said, winking at me.

I smiled. "True."

"You were obviously preoccupied."

"I'm just here trying to find something for my mother's birthday. I usually buy her jewelry or something for the house, but this time she specifically said she wanted a new outfit."

"And so you were left with the task of finding the perfect one."

"Exactly."

"How old is she? If you don't mind me asking?"

"Not at all. She'll be fifty, but she's going on twenty. So whatever I find has to be trendy enough for her to wear, but not so trendy that my father will have a fit over it."

Monique laughed. "I got you. Classy, not trashy."

"Exactly. Chic, stylish; not too old, not too young. Like yourself, my mother's got skills."

I couldn't stop staring at her. She was a natural sister with natural beauty that didn't require make-up. Her poise was confident, like she knew she was the shit, yet she didn't flaunt it for the entire world to see. I should have been less obvious with my flirtation, but damn it, she was just too damned fine and at that moment, smooth was just something that I couldn't be.

"So where's your wife or girlfriend? She should be here to help you."

I had to struggle to keep my smile to a minimum when she said that. Obviously, I wasn't the only one doing some shameless flirting.

"I don't have either. I'm all alone in this cruel world of women's clothing."

She raised an eyebrow and said, "Well, baby, don't take this the wrong way, but from the looks of what you have in your hand, I'd say you're going to need some help."

"You think so, huh? Maybe I should go for some stripes and polka dots instead?"

"Uh, no. Tell you what. Why don't I help you?"

"Sounds like a good idea," I said.

"Before we get started, why don't you put those clothes down before they kick you out of the store and me—for standing beside you."

My two-hour tour of duty easily turned into an all-day affair as Monique and I went from store to store, in search of the hippest fifty-year-old's outfit we could find. Monique chose the baddest of ensembles, but I didn't let her know that, as I found a way to find fault with everything she chose, while I made sure we got to know each other better. We eventually chose a silk blouse low-cut enough to reveal a touch of cleavage, and a black skirt that would rest just above her knees to show a pair of legs she's proud of. My pops was probably going to have a heart attack, but it was all good because before we left the mall, I had Monique's number, which I didn't hesitate to use the next day.

"So, did your mother like her gift?"

"My father didn't, but yeah, she loved it. She said she was surprised I had such good taste."

"Oh, do you?" Monique asked.

I lowered my voice to a sexy baritone. "Yeah, I do."

We had dinner later that night, and we officially started dating two weeks later. Monique and I connected so well that it was hard to imagine a time when she wasn't my woman. We became best friends and great lovers as we complemented each other in every way.

I was feeling Monique like I'd never felt any female before. She was real and kept it real, and I did the same, which was why I never kept Jalisa a secret. From the start I let Monique know that I was a father and that my little girl came first. I also explained the whole frustrating situation with Tina. I didn't want to hide that from her either. Just like I'd suspected, she had no problem with Jalisa, and she told me about how she'd dealt with a couple of Tinas in her lifetime.

I felt blessed to have finally met a woman I could relax around. I eventually took her over to my parents' place. I wanted them to meet the woman who was being seriously considered for the role of Mrs. Randy Lincoln. She and my mother hit it off from the start, which I knew they would. My pops was more than pleased. I introduced Monique to Jalisa six months later. I waited that long because I wanted to make sure that we were on the right track. Just like she did with my parents, Monique immediately clicked with Jalisa. It was almost hard to believe she didn't have any kids of her own the way she carried on with my little girl. That was a big reliever for me, because there'd been other women who didn't get along with Jalisa in the past, which was why I was no longer with them. Everything was working out for me. I had a beautiful little girl and a sexy, intelligent woman at my side. My future was looking damn bright.

And then the migraines started.

Out of the blue, Tina, who couldn't seem to stand me before, suddenly came to the realization that I was her soul mate. Of course, I knew her change of heart was because of my growing relationship with Monique. I think up until that point, she thought I was going to come crawling back to her, begging for her to take me back. Once that didn't happen I think she suddenly realized what she'd lost when she'd decided to sleep around with her former agent behind my back.

At first Monique let Tina's meddling roll off her back. Like I said, Tina wasn't the first pain in the ass she'd dealt with, and baby mama drama wasn't new to her. She'd gone through similar circumstances herself, so she knew how to deal with

Tina's little comments or her unexpected visits to my place. But as time passed, and Tina's persistence increased, the inevitable started to happen: our relationship began to suffer. It just became too hard for Monique to ignore Tina's unfriendly attitude toward her and the way she blatantly threw herself at me. As Tina had undoubtedly hoped, Monique and I started to argue. She couldn't understand why I accepted Tina's nonsense. Why I let Tina call whenever she wanted. Why I never put her in check when she was out of line. Why, when Jalisa was with Tina for the summer, she still found it necessary to call me.

"Why is she calling? She has Jalisa with her. What could she possibly need?"

"Baby, don't worry about her. She just wanted to let me know what time they would be arriving next week."

"At one o'clock in the morning?"

"It's only seven o'clock in Italy."

"And she knows what time it is here. Come on, Randy. Why don't you put a stop to her shit? You know what she's doing. She knows what she's doing."

"Baby, everything's fine. There's nothing to worry about."

"Right. And maybe one day she and I could be friends."

"I wouldn't allow that. I need you just the way you are—untainted."

"Then why do you allow her to do what she's doing? I know you don't tell me everything she says to you. But I know she's saying something you don't like, or don't want to hear. I can read it in your face."

"Monique, I'll handle Tina, Okay?"

"When? I'm getting tired of her calling whenever she wants to. I'm tired of her little surprise visits. And damn it, if she gives me one more smart-ass comment, or look, I'm going to slap some ugly on her."

"Baby, can't we all just get along?"

"I'm not joking."

And she wasn't, either. Because the following week when Tina brought Jalisa home, she did what she normally did, and Monique did exactly as she promised. She smacked Tina so hard, I know the makeup artists had a field day trying to cover up her bruise. I couldn't blame Monique, though, because Tina deserved it. But it all happened in front of Jalisa, and even though Tina was Tina, she was still Jalisa's mother.

"What the hell was that about?" I'd asked Monique. I had to confront her about it, because I didn't want it happening again.

"I told you what I would do if she gave me another comment."

"Yeah, you did, but damn Monique, use some common sense. You didn't have to do that in front of Jalisa."

"Common sense? Common sense would be to tell that bitch that she is Jalisa's mother and that's it. Common sense would be to make her understand that you want nothing to do with her other than when she comes for her daughter, who she had no problem disrespecting me in front of. I'm tired of her shit, Randy! And frankly, I'm getting tired of you playing her little game."

"Game? Who the hell is playing games?"

"You! Every time she calls or comes by, you play Mr. Softy with her. What? Are you incapable of saying 'Leave me the fuck alone'? And don't tell me she doesn't want you. I can read her thoughts, because she puts them out there for me to see in plain sight."

"Come on Monique, we've gone over this before. You need to stop worrying. She doesn't want me."

"Bullshit. I'm a woman. I know these things."

"Right, you are a woman. And you are bigger than she is. And so what if Tina wants me. I'm with you, and I damn sure don't want her."

"Then get it through her thick, weave-wearing, head."

"There's no need to."

"Randy, I know the body language. I know how to read in between the lines. You don't have to admit anything to me if you don't want to."

"Monique, listen—"

"I don't want to listen. I don't want to talk about this anymore. I'm sorry about slapping her in front of Jalisa. I really am. And I'll apologize to Jalisa. But I will not continue to put up with Tina's shit. And if you don't want to try and do something about it, then I don't want to put up with yours either."

"Monique—"

Before I could get another word out, she stormed out. That was the last argument we had. And since then, Tina's called me on my cell phone—thankfully. But this last time, Monique was sitting right next to me when it went off. And of course when I didn't answer, she wanted to know why.

"Why didn't you answer your phone?"

"It wasn't anyone important," I said.

She looked at my phone and said, "Hmmph. It was important enough for them to leave a voice mail."

"I'll check it later."

"Right. Later."

Damn.

Monique

Iknew who the call was from. He should have just taken the damn call, instead of avoiding it and trying to play it off as if I were fool enough to believe his pathetic lie about it being no one important. His actions showed me that the suspicions I'd had, had some merit behind them. Had the call been innocent, he would have had no problem answering it. But he didn't, and that could only mean that Tina was definitely out to steal my man. Well, here's what I had to say about that.

If she wanted him, she could have him.

I mean, I loved Randy to death, but I just couldn't continue to stand by and watch Tina play her little mind games with him. More importantly, I refused to be ridiculed by her. Oh no! I definitely wasn't having that. So if Randy wanted to be baited by her, then fine. In love or not, I was getting tired of all of the stress anyway.

Before I met Randy, stressful relationships were all I knew. I dated one fine caramel brother who put Shemar Moore to shame with his looks. I mean

16   *Dwayne S. Joseph*

Ivan had it going on. He had pretty-boy looks, with eyelashes to die for. His body had to have been sculpted from the Super Black Man catalogue. And best of all, he made love like he invented it. Brother was so smooth with his, that he had my peaches and cream overflowing. Unfortunately, looks and sex were all he had going for himself, because months into the relationship, I quickly discovered that he couldn't keep a job to save his life. And when it came to career goals, he had no clue as to what they were. Worst yet, as soon as he realized I was making a nice-sized salary, he became a leech trying his damndest to survive off of all of the long hours I put into my job. I got rid of him quickly, but the damage had been done: time and energy had been wasted.

My next pleasure trip was with Derek. He wasn't the prettiest of brothers, but at least he had a steady job, and was a great conversationalist. After six months, I learned to look past his beady eyes, his crooked smile, and his flared nostrils, and take him for what he was—a nice, hardworking black man. Only problem with Derek was that he forgot to mention to me that he had six kids to four different women, and enough baby mama drama to make Carl Weber proud. Thankfully, I never let him have a piece of me.

I dated a few others here and there, but like all the rest, they gave me nothing but grief. I soon developed the mind-set that men couldn't hold a job, couldn't keep their zippers from falling down, couldn't tell the truth, didn't know what it meant to make love, and didn't understand that the world didn't revolve around them. I was frustrated and intent on avoiding the whole relationship pit, so when I met Randy, the last thing I expected was to fall head over heels for him.

I was in the mall shopping, when he literally ran into me, nearly sending me to the ground to join the bags I'd been holding. I was in a foul mood that day. I'd just lost a case earlier that morning, and my client had to go to jail for three years simply because his friend decided to rob a 7-Eleven while he waited in the car. He was in the wrong place at the wrong time, and to his "good" fortune, they were in my client's car. His friend shot the cashier behind the counter, almost killing him. That had been the nail in the coffin. They were arrested, and my client, who happened to be my girlfriend's little brother, became an accomplice to the crime.

Needless to say, Randy bumping into me was not what I needed at the time, because I was already ticking and ready to blow. And that's just what I was about to do until I looked up and made eye contact with him. As God was my witness, I swear I was almost at a loss for words; that's how fine Randy was. And it wasn't just his looks. I mean yes, he did have an intense pair of deep-set chocolate-brown, bedroom eyes. And yes, his lips were so Boris Kodjoe fine that I wanted to stretch up on my tiptoes and sample them for days. And okay, his build was all man—broad shoulders and thick arms—both major turn-ons for me. But what truly made him one of the handsomest men I'd ever laid my eyes on was his style. Everything was just right. The Brooks Brothers suit he wore was expensive and tailored, and didn't hide the fact that he was a regular at a gym. The jewelry he had on—a silver bracelet and silver chain with a cross hanging from it—were both simple, unlike the gaudy pieces most men like to wear these days. He was well groomed with a faded goatee connected to his sideburns. And instead of cornrows, his hair was cut low and tapered at the sides. Best of all, with his back straight and his chest out, his posture reeked confidence and professionalism, and that was a big plus in my book, because as far as I'm concerned, there is nothing worse than a man with bad posture.

Completely taken by the complete package standing in front of me, I didn't say anything for a few short seconds, but instead stared at Randy and thought to myself that there was just something about him that felt familiar and right. Finally, when I opened my mouth to speak, instead of exploding like I was going to do, I did something that was out of character for me: I flirted. To make a long story short, Randy flirted back and we ended up spending the rest of the day together. The next evening we met up for dinner.

It was nice to have a stimulating conversation with a man who had it going on, yet didn't desire to be the main topic. We spoke about our jobs, politics, movies, sports—everything. We talked until the restaurant closed, and after that he drove me back to my house in Queens, and since it was mid-July and the nighttime air was just right, we talked for another hour outside. As our night came to an end, he gave me a hug and a very soft, sweet kiss. Then he dropped a semi-bomb on me.

"Before this goes any further," he said with the

most serious of stares, "I have to let you know, I have a four-year-old daughter. I'm telling you this because my daughter's very much a part of my life. I'm hoping that this won't be a turn-off for you, but if it is, I understand."

At first I was a little apprehensive, because of having been in those situations before, but I was really into him, and after he explained the whole situation to me, which included telling me about Tina, I realized just how much of a "real" man he was. I told him I was okay with his situation and agreed to see him again. Two weeks passed before anything became official between us.

I couldn't remember having as much fun with anyone as I did with Randy. We were like teenagers experiencing love for the first time. In a sense, it was kind of like my first time, because I had never felt that way about any man before. I couldn't get enough of him. And when I wasn't with him, he was still with me in my thoughts. We spent as much time together as we possibly could. The only time we were truly apart was when he had Jalisa on the weekends. But even then we spent those nights together on the phone. We experienced sunsets and sunrises with the receivers glued to our ears.

We did that for a good six months before the day came when I finally got to meet Jalisa. I was as nervous as I could ever remember. I wanted to connect with her, but I was prepared for a chilly reception. After all, I was the outsider, and I was sure that in her eyes, I was probably trying to take her daddy away. I guess because I had been so disillusioned by the lovers of my past, I never really gave any thought to having any kids of my own. But with Randy I'd begun to think about it, and I knew that how I dealt with Jalisa was probably going to be the measuring stick he was going to use to determine if I would be a good mother or not; something I was unsure about.

So I went with him to pick her up from her mother's house.

"Now before we go, remember, Tina can be weird sometimes. And if she acts funny towards you, don't sweat it. Just let it roll and ignore her like I do."

"Don't worry, baby," I reassured him. "Everything will be fine."

Damn, was I wrong.

Everything wasn't fine.

Especially after Tina opened the door.

Now I'm sure she was attractive and deserved to be a model, but on that day, she was as ugly as ugly could be. She gave me the nastiest glare when Randy introduced me. I tried not to let it get to me, so I just ignored her little "humph," and extended my hand to her. Damn if the bitch didn't take it. She pouted her lips, looked away from me to Randy, and then turned her back and called for Jalisa. When Jalisa came to the door with backpack in hand, I sighed. All two feet of her jumped into Randy's outstretched arms, and gave him the biggest kiss.

"Daddy!" She was the spitting image of Randy, except she had wide, permanently frightened eyes, almost like Tina's.

"How's my little munchkin?"

"Fine. Who's that?" she asked, pointing at me.

Before he could introduce me, Tina took the

opportunity to make sure one thing stood perfectly clear. She took Jalisa from Randy's arms, put her back down, stared back at me and said to Randy, "Take care of *my* little girl." Then she bent down, gave Jalisa a hug and with her leveled up at me, said, "Now remember, honey, no talking to strangers. If you don't know them, then they don't need to know you."

I took hold of Randy's hand and gave it a light squeeze because I could tell he was about to say something. The last thing I wanted was to have an ugly scene break out right then and there with Jalisa standing silently looking at me. It's bad enough she was probably wondering why the "stranger" was clenching and unclenching her fist.

Take Jalisa out of the picture and I could have slapped Tina, no questions asked. But instead, I turned around and walked away down the hallway to the elevator. When Randy, with Jalisa skipping in tow came, I simply looked at him and shook my head. He shrugged his shoulders, gave me an I-warned-you look and pressed the button for an elevator.

While we waited, Jalisa tugged on my pants leg and looked up at me with the most adorable brown eyes. She smiled, and in a voice as sweet as sugar, said, "Don't worry, Daddy told me you weren't a stranger."

I melted and said, "Oh, he did?"

Jalisa nodded her head like she had trouble balancing it on her neck. "Yup."

I put out my hand. "Well in that case, I'm Monique."

She took my hand with her own little fingers. "I'm Jalisa."

"That's such a pretty name."

"Yup. My daddy thinks so too."

"Well, he's right."

Jalisa giggled out loud and then hid her face behind her hands. "Yoooou can't seeee meeee!"

I gasped and said, "Randy, Jalisa disappeared. Get the police."

The little angel removed her hands and smiled her father's smile. "It's okay. I'm right here." She giggled again, and any feelings of anger I may have had quickly went away. When we got on the elevator, Jalisa's hand was in mine. We bonded that first day, and after that everything was cake.

Except when it came to Tina.

After our first encounter, nothing got better between us. And little by little, she made sure to do whatever she could to interfere with the relationship Randy and I had. Whether she had Jalisa or not, she would stop by Randy's apartment unexpected and unwanted.

"I was in the neighborhood and I thought I'd— oh, *she's* here."

She.

That's who I was. She never used my name. Finally, one day, I had had enough.

"That's right, Tina. I am here. And just in case you forgot, the name is Monique. Use it."

"Is *she* talking to me, Randy? I know *she's* not talking to me with that tone. *She* better not be, because I will be all up in *her* face."

Before I could say a word, Randy took her out into the hallway and closed the front door. I don't know what he told her, but all I heard was, "bitch!" Ooh, that set me off. I quickly opened the door ready to pull out some hair, but instead of the cat-fight, I watched, with smoke coming from her ears, as Tina stormed down the hall and into the elevator.

"Please tell me Miss Thing didn't call me a bitch."

"I told you she was nuts."

"Oh no, she does not know me to be disrespecting me like that. I may look nice, but believe me, I have a whole lot of ugly wanting to come out on her flat ass."

And believe me, I did. Tina worked my first, second, and last nerve. To make matters worse, as her modeling took off, her head grew right with it, which gave her an even greater-than-thou attitude. It was impossible for us to be in the same room. Hell, the city almost wasn't big enough.

"Baby, do you think you can try to keep your claws in when Tina brings Jalisa by?"

"Keep my claws in? You're asking the wrong woman to stay composed. Why don't you just do something about her, Randy? I'm getting tired of having to be the calm one when she comes around. I'm at the end of my rope with her."

"I'll deal with her, okay? Just remember that she's not all there. Besides, she's going to be traveling a lot, which means that you won't have to deal with her as much."

"We'll see."

For the first couple of months, Randy was right. The more Tina traveled, the less stress I felt. We eventually moved into an apartment together, and since my relationship with Jalisa was outstanding, I looked forward to having her around. I became like a second mother to her, which I'm sure she didn't mind, because she didn't get the full attention she deserved from Tina anyway. I later found out that Randy felt the same way I did.

"Baby, I want to ask you something." Randy said.

"What is it?"

"I'm not going to beat around the bush with you, okay? I'm just going to come straight out and ask."

"Okay."

"You know I love you, right?"

"I thought you weren't going to beat around the bush."

"Right. Well . . . you know how much having you in my life means to me, don't you?"

"Is that what you wanted to ask me? Or is this going somewhere I didn't pack my bags for?"

"What would you say if I said I wanted full custody of Jalisa?"

"Full custody? Are you serious?"

"Yes I am. Now I know that you and Tina can't, and probably won't ever get along—"

"Damn right."

"I also know that by having Jalisa here all the time, Tina will probably be even nastier toward you, but I just don't like the idea of my little girl living amongst that whole modeling scene. Besides, with Tina's status getting bigger and bigger, it's going to mean that she would have to travel more than she already is, which means that she's either going to have to take Jalisa, or bring her here."

"Which is never a problem."

"No, it isn't. I know this is a big deal. That's why I wanted to approach you first. I'm not trying to force motherhood on you or make you uncomfortable. I just don't want my little girl going from school to school or getting her education from tutors. And right now, I don't see Tina giving up her career for Jalisa."

"No, she certainly wouldn't do that."

"Can you at least take a couple of days to think about it? I want to know how you feel about this. Think about it and let me know. I won't do it if you—"

"Randy, you should do it. I know how much Jalisa means to you, and you know I adore her. Living here would be a hell of a lot better than her living with Tina."

"You know Tina won't like this, right?"

"Baby, call her right now and tell her. I'll grab the other phone so I can listen in."

I did just that too. I listened to Tina go off and start spitting curse words left and right. Of course she mentioned my name.

"Was this that bitch's idea?"

"Tina, my decision had nothing to do with her."

"Whatever. I will not have that bitch raise my daughter. I will not let you have my little girl."

"I'm trying to do what's best for *our* little girl. I don't want her having to switch schools. I don't want her living around the superficial people you deal with. And she's going to need someone there with her. You won't be able to."

"I'll hire a nanny."

"I won't have some strange woman raising my daughter."

"Then keep your trick away from her!"

Trick?

It wasn't easy, but I kept my mouth shut and

listened, enjoying every minute of her displeasure. I only wish I could have seen the look on her face.

Unfortunately, my pleasure was short-lived, because the custody battle was ugly. Tina accused me of trying to turn Jalisa against her; she made up lies about me bad-mouthing Jalisa. She also accused me of trying to brainwash Jalisa by constantly telling her what a bad mother Tina was, which was actually true, but never relayed to Jalisa.

Fortunately, the judge had common sense enough to not buy Tina's stories, and when everything was all said and done, Tina was only allowed to have Jalisa for four months out of the year.

When Jalisa finally moved in with us permanently, things calmed down a little. I guess the reality of the situation finally sunk into Tina's thick head. Of course, that didn't stop her from trying to get under my skin. She did anything she could to annoy me.

When she came by, I got looks.

When she called, I got comments.

I tried to be the better person, and to ignore her immature and oftentimes ghetto behavior, because she just wasn't worth my time. But sometimes that was damn near impossible. And finally the day came when impossible became possible, and I just couldn't hold myself back. She had come back from another photo shoot to get Jalisa, and when I answered the door, attitude was what greeted me.

"Humph. Do you always have to be here? Where's Randy? And where's my little girl?"

I was already PMSing that day, so I didn't have

the patience for her jealous, immature shit. "Tina, why do you always have a stick up your ass?"

"Excuse me?"

"There is no excuse. You need to grow up and be a woman, and be a better example for Jalisa. Stop showing her attitude and ugliness."

"Don't you even try to tell me how to raise my daughter. I noticed she's picking up some bad habits. They're probably from you."

"So being a polite, sweet little girl with manners is bad?"

"Where's Jalisa? Jalisa! Come here. Now!"

When Jalisa came, her eyes were puffy, and I could tell that she had been crying. That broke my heart. I bent down and gave her a hug and kiss on her cheek. My heart went out to her. She deserved better than Tina. Before I could even finish the word *good-bye,* Tina grabbed Jalisa and snatched her away from me.

"I don't care what you do with anyone else, but when it comes to my daughter, bitch, you better never let me see you do that again."

I couldn't take it anymore. I had had enough. I stood up so fast and hit her under her eye so hard, my hand numbed up. Although it felt too good to release some of my pent-up tension, I regretted my actions right away, because Jalisa started crying immediately. To make matters worse, Randy, who'd been in the shower, heard Tina screaming and Jalisa crying, and rushed out of the bathroom with his towel wrapped around him.

"What the hell is going on?"

"That stupid bitch hit me! I'm going to bruise! Bitch, I will sue your ass."

I shouldn't have responded, but my tongue couldn't be held. "Call me a bitch again Tina, and I'll give you a matching bruise on the other side."

Without another word, Tina grabbed Jalisa by her shirt collar and stormed away. Before the elevator closed, I heard her yell, "bitch!"

When Randy closed the door, we had it out.

And then I stormed out.

I was pissed at him, and I was also pissed at myself. I hated snapping like that in front of Jalisa, but Tina's nasty attitude had just broken through the last bit of lining my composure had left.

Randy and I didn't argue much after that. As a matter of fact, we barely spoke to each other over the next few days. Thankfully, I didn't hear Tina's voice for a few weeks after, because she stopped calling.

The house, that is.

I knew that she hadn't actually stopped calling, because Randy's cell phone started ringing more and more. On one occasion, he was in the shower when his phone went off. It was twelve o'clock in the morning, so I knew it couldn't have been work-related. I knew that there was only one person it could have been, and when I checked the caller ID, I saw that I was right. I never let on to Randy that I knew she was calling him. I tried to ignore it. But when we went out the other night, and his phone rang and he didn't answer it, that was the last straw. I'm a woman and I knew what she was trying to do. Whether he wanted her or not, his reluctance to put her in check set me on fire. He could be her fool all he wanted. I wanted out.

Abe

"Give me another fifteen minutes and I'll really give you something to smile about."

"Believe me, Taki, if I had fifteen more minutes to spare, and another pair of boxers with me, it would be on."

"You were incredible today, Abe. I can still feel you inside of me."

"That's what I like to hear."

"Ten more minutes?" Taki begged, placing her hand over my crotch.

It wasn't easy to do, but I grabbed ahold of her hand and pulled it away from my hardening member. "We both need to get home, Taki."

"Five more minutes?" she said, grabbing hold of me again with her other hand. "Put it in. Give me a few good, hard thrusts, and then pull it out. I want to feel you inside of me again."

"Don't get greedy, Taki," I said, pulling her other hand away, which had nearly succeeded in getting my zipper all the way down. "Being greedy will only ruin things."

Taki moaned and nibbled on my earlobe. "It's hard to not be greedy, Abe," she said with a whisper.

"But it's better to be safe than sorry."

Taki groaned. "I'm tired of being safe."

"But for your kids you will be."

Taki sighed. "I know."

"Get home," I said. "I'll see you tomorrow."

"Okay," she said reluctantly.

We kissed for a few seconds and then got in our cars and drove away to go back to our separate lives.

Things were starting to change. Well, Taki was. I'd been noticing it the past few times we'd been together, but really saw it this time. The longer, tighter hugs. The lingering of her lips on mine for far longer than they should have. The look in her eyes that no longer growled, "Come and fuck me," but now whispered, "Come and lay with me." I had hoped this wouldn't happen. Taki had caught feelings.

I tightened my grip around my steering wheel and clenched my jaws. I'd been seeing Taki for a little over seven months. We'd first made eye contact at a company Christmas party. She'd been there with her husband, Whilice. I was there with my wife, Nakyia. Taki was working in a different department at the time, but a month after the party, she was promoted to be the head of the entire East Coast region of advertising. I began working under her a month after that.

Everything was on the up-and-up in the beginning. We were both two very driven individuals who took pride in creating television and print-ad campaigns that drove consumers toward the client's product. Taki and I made a great team. With her visual skills and my flair for creating catchy slogans and witty dialogue, companies were practically battling for us to render our services.

Like I said, in the beginning our relationship was strictly business. I won't lie and say that we never flirted or exchanged glances here and there, because we did. But we were both married, so we never let the flirtation go too far. But one day out of the blue, sitting in her office trying to come up with an ad campaign for a Latino-owned clothing company, without warning, Taki changed the dynamics of our relationship.

I was in mid-sentence reciting a slogan I'd come up with when Taki reached across the table we'd been sitting by and placed her lips against mine. Taken by surprise, I pulled back almost immediately. Almost. I won't lie; I did take a moment to taste the cherry lipstick she'd been wearing. But it had only been a moment.

"What was that about?"

Taki looked at me for a few short seconds and licked her lips sensuously before she said, "One of us had to make the move."

"The move?"

"Yes."

"What do you mean?"

"You know what I mean, Abe."

I clenched my jaws for a second and then nodded. She was right; I did know.

"This was going to happen sooner or later," she

said. "There was no point in delaying the inevitable. I'm actually surprised that you didn't move first."

"You're married," I said, thinking about all of the times I'd imagined doing just that.

"So are you," Taki countered.

"You're also my boss," I said. "The whole Michael Douglas, Demi Moore scenario isn't one I'd like to experience."

"Trust me, Abe . . . I may be finer than Demi, but I am nowhere near as crazy as her character was."

I flashed a slight smile. Half-Asian, half-black, with an Angela Bassett physique, Lauryn Hill lips, and eyes that could make the gayest of men turn straight, I had to agree: Demi in her heyday couldn't touch Taki on her worst.

I stroked my goatee. "Demi didn't lose her mind until Mike gave it to her," I said.

Taki smirked. "Are you saying you'll make me lose my mind, Abe?"

I shook my head. "I'm just saying that Demi was sane until she got dicked down."

Taki's eyes closed a bit as she nibbled down on her bottom lip. "Are you going to dick me down?" she asked, coming around the table and standing in front of me. "Is that what you plan to do? Make me crazy? Do you have skills like that?"

Taki traced a finely manicured index finger down my cheek to my chest, and then down to my crotch. My hand found its way beneath both her blouse and bra. "In my twenty-eight years," I said, squeezing her erect nipple, "I've never had any complaints. And I've always had requests for thirds and fourths."

Taki let out a slow breath and moaned. "But will you make me go crazy?" she asked, pulling my zipper down, slipping past my boxers and grabbing hold of me.

I closed my eyes and got chills as she stroked.

"You're so big, Abe," Taki whispered.

"Still want to know if I'll make you crazy?" I asked as my tongue did circles around her nipple now.

"Since I first laid my eyes on you at the company party," Taki said breathlessly.

No need for further conversation, Taki and I undressed and then fucked on top of the work we had spread out across the round, sturdy table. I answered Taki's question with every deep, hard thrust. Answered it so good that she demanded I go deeper, harder, faster, until she orgasmed.

When we were finished, Taki took a finger, dipped it in the semen I'd spilled across her stomach, and took that finger into her mouth. "Good answer," she said with a seductive smile.

Wiping myself off with my T-shirt, I asked the first question that popped into my mind when I released. "You don't plan on doing a Demi to me now, do you, boss?"

"Cut the *boss* bullshit," Taki said. "I told you, I'm not crazy. But . . ." she paused, licked her lips, and then said, "your dick is good."

Things were never the same after that.

Never letting the pleasure come before the business, Taki and I fucked whenever and wherever we could. In her office. In mine. In the backseat of her car. In the front seat of mine. At a hotel. Sometimes on the way there.

I know I should have felt guilty about what was going on. After all, my wife, Nakyia, was a beautiful woman. Five-five and slender, yet thick in all of the right places. Beautiful brown eyes to go with her smooth, coffee-colored skin. Short, Toni Braxton hairstyle to compliment her soft, round face. Educated with the perfect combination of book and common sense; I'd be hard-pressed to find a woman as complete as Nakyia was.

Being riddled with guilt is definitely something that I should have been, but I wasn't. See, as perfect as Nakyia was, there was just one imperfect thing about her. Something that was completely out of her control.

Two years before Taki came into the picture, Nakyia was afflicted with trigeminal neuralgia, which is a disorder of the fifth cranial, or trigeminal, nerve that causes episodes of intense, stabbing, electric shock-like pain in the areas of the face where the branches of the nerve are distributed. Lips, eyes, nose, scalp, forehead, upper and lower jaw; the whole right side of her face was affected. Universally considered to be one of the most painful afflictions known to man, trigeminal neuralgia isn't fatal, but it is an extremely painful and life-changing disorder.

Because of the constant pain she was in, the intimacy in our marriage disappeared. We couldn't caress the same, couldn't kiss with the same passion as we used to. Worst of all, the sex changed. One minute Nakyia would be fine and the next minute, she'd be damn near tears from the pain searing through the right side of her face.

It was frustrating to watch the woman I loved suffer, and not be able to do anything about it. So frustrating, that after a while, I completely gave up on trying to have any intimacy at all. With the distance the neuralgia caused, we went from living together as husband and wife, to nothing more than roommates who occasionally slept together in the same bed. And I say *occasionally* because I spent many nights out on the couch because it was just too damned hard to be in the same bed without being able to touch her.

I know that to a lot of people my affair with Taki was just plain wrong. After all, Nakyia was suffering. She was the one forced to take medicine four times a day with little relief. She was the one who couldn't talk without feeling pain, couldn't eat without feeling pain, couldn't walk without the wind blowing on her face and causing her to cringe and clench her jaws as she fought tears and willed the pain to go away.

She was the one who had trigeminal neuralgia. Not me.

I was just the bystander, and having an affair was just about the lowest thing to do. Bystander or not, I vowed through sickness and health and I was supposed to be the rock for Nakyia to lean on. That's what anyone standing on the outside looking in would say, and they would be right. Cheating was wrong.

But until they've walked in my shoes, they would never understand how doing the wrong thing was something that I desperately needed to do, because they would never be able to fully grasp the depths of my frustration over not being able to kiss or caress my wife without the knowledge that the pleasure I was trying to bring her could and oftentimes did bring her nothing but pain.

But our sex life or better yet, lack of one, wasn't the only thing that pushed me into another woman's arms. Four times a day, every day, Nakyia had no choice but to take medication, just so that she could function on a somewhat normal level. Because of the medicine, she developed some nasty mood swings, and most of the time I did whatever I could to avoid being around her. But even when she was almost herself, and I wanted nothing more than to just be by her side, nothing for us was normal. We rarely went out in public together or hung out with friends because she felt embarrassed by her condition. We couldn't do normal things like take showers together, because the water hitting her face would cause her pain. We couldn't laugh together the same way we used to, because she could never just let go.

Nothing was the same for us anymore.

Like I said, cheating was wrong and I knew it. But I'm human. And as the distance between Nakyia and I grew wider, I began to get lonely. I missed the affection. I missed the excitement of being a couple in love with nothing but the usual worries. When Taki laid that kiss on me as much I wanted to fight it, the urge to be physical without holding back was just too strong, and I enjoyed all that Taki had to give and gave her all that she could take.

The regret never came.
And I only wanted more.

As I drove home, I thought about the arrangement Taki and I had made. We agreed to satisfy each other's urges, and for however long we had, give each other the attention neither of us got at home, without expectations.

No strings attached in the truest form.

I tightened my grip around my steering wheel even harder and blew out a frustrated breath of air through my nostrils. Taki had caught feelings and I was going to have to change that. I was happy with the arrangement we had and I saw no reason for a change.

Taki

I wanted to ask him again to stay longer, but I knew he wasn't going to give in. The one rule we had was that no matter what, we wouldn't change what we were doing or the way we were doing it, because things were going too well for us. Why fix something that wasn't broken, right? He was right and I knew it; breaking our rule wouldn't have been a good idea. But damn it, it was hard to not want to do just that.

Without Abe I was an unlit matchstick. Stiff and dry. But with him, I was alive and burning. He was the spark that ignited me in ways my own husband couldn't. With Abe, I never had to worry about faking an orgasm, because from the moment he laid his hands on me, I was wet and ready to explode. It was surreal the way he made my body feel. He seemed to know my trigger zones better than I did.

Ten years behind us, and my husband Whilice still fumbled around my body like a clumsy teenager unsure of what to do next. I know sex

isn't everything, but damn, is a little skill and satisfaction too much to ask for?

Whilice wasn't completely dissatisfying when we
first met. Fresh out of Florida University with my
degree in hand, I was ready to take the advertising
world by storm. With the chips doubly stacked
against me as a minority and a female, I knew that
if I wanted to make my mark, I was going to have
to bull my way in and prove that I wasn't just a
pretty face with a shapely figure. I had to be headstrong, determined, driven, and downright ruth-
less at times.

Whilice was that way when I met him.

I was on the hunt for a new Mazda when we met.
Whilice was the head salesman at the Lakeland AutoMall, the biggest car dealership around in
Florida at the time. It was obvious by all the
plaques and awards in his office that he knew the
game well. Back then, Whilice had it going on. He
was tall with dimples and sweet brown eyes to
match his dark chocolate skin. He was also bald,
which was a very big turn-on for me.

For the better part of two hours, I dragged
Whilice down every aisle of the AutoMall, looking
at cars I had absolutely no interest in. He intrigued
me. He was tall, fine, could wear the hell out of a
suit, and his career was obviously in high gear. That
was another turn-on for me: he was driven to be a
success. While we walked through the lot, we got
to know a lot about one another, and by the time
my shopping excursion was over, we'd exchanged
phone numbers. I also left the lot in a brand new-
Mazda 626.

It wasn't until a week later before we'd gone out

on our first date. Six months after that, we were married, and had our first child, Jayme, three months later.

In the beginning, Whilice was a caring and sensitive man who catered to my needs and wants, and for the first couple of years of our marriage, I was fulfilled. So much so, that I never really let the fact that he was somewhat disappointing in bed bother me. I just made the best of with what he could do, and when he fell asleep, grabbed my vibrator from my drawer, went into the bathroom and took care of myself. This I did more times than I would have liked to, but hey, when in a marriage, you have to accept the good with the bad. At least that's what my mother always told me.

So I did just that. Accepted. Had two more kids—Veronica and Devin—within three years, and accepted some more. Disappointing sex or not, we were a complete modern-day upper-middle-class family, with a beautiful house, great jobs, and two cars. We were happy. Hell, I was happy.

But then our roles changed.

Selling cars left and right, Whilice was always the breadwinner. But as the economy got worse, my salary increased, while his went in the opposite direction. Once the best salesman in the region, his sales dropped dramatically, and oftentimes his paychecks would be less than half of what they used to be. Knowing how driven my husband was, and seeing for myself how successful he had been, I had no doubt that it was just a matter of time before he would tame the wild bull that kept throwing him off. Without fussing and without worrying, I rode the wave and waited for the tide to change.

Unfortunately, it never did.

Letting himself go physically, it just seemed as though he'd become content with making spare change. I held on for as long as I could, but the more he settled and became physically unappealing, the more I needed an escape. Ultimately, I couldn't take it anymore, and I ended up having my first affair when I went away on a business trip.

I met him at the bar in the hotel I was staying in. He was attractive, had a fine build, and after a couple of drinks, I had a nice buzz and was horny. Later that night, we took full advantage of the clean sheets in the room. The fling was meaningless for me, but the sexual release was necessary, because for the first time in a long time, I didn't need my Silver Bullet.

I didn't have another affair again, until I met Abe. I fought it for as long as I could because I really didn't want to be unfaithful again. I wasn't happy, but I had morals. I also didn't want to break my own rule about interoffice relationships. They were always a no-no in my book. I didn't want that kind of taboo. But the more I worked with Abe, the more I wanted to feel him. I was attracted to not only his physique, but his mind as well. He was as focused as I was. Working alongside him was like playing a chess match. And because I was the head honcho, I had to use my mind and make sure I stayed at the top of the game.

I handled myself well, until I kissed him. We were working late in my office, and that night, I just couldn't take it anymore. His scent had me wet, and I was tired of fighting the obvious. I also knew the attraction was mutual, because I saw him catching glimpses of my body whenever he could. I made the first move, though, because I wanted the control. I wanted it known that it happened because I made it happen. Before the kiss, I rationalized in my head that a onetime fuck wasn't going to hurt. If anything, with the release of the sexual tension, we'd be able to get back to focusing on only the work. The only problem was I didn't expect to become so hooked. And never did I think I would be falling in love. That was one monkey wrench I didn't anticipate. It was also the one thing that I didn't know how to get rid of.

I pulled the car into the driveway and sat still for a moment. I had to put my loving mother, happy wife face on. This wasn't always easy for me. Lying to Whilice was one thing, because I really wasn't happy, but lying to my kids was a different beast altogether. They were everything to me, and likewise I was to them. I was their mommy who could do no wrong. Sometimes I wondered about what it would do to them if they were to ever find out about my affair. How would they react? At ten, our oldest child, Jayme, would be old enough to understand what I was doing was wrong. She adores Whilice. Actually, all of our girls do. He may be an underachiever when it comes to his professional career, but when it comes to them, he works hard at being the best father he can be. That's one thing I've always liked about him. With Whilice, family was always his priority.

Jayme is just like him. She has the same happy-go-lucky attitude that he has. She rarely gets mad, and is not as aggressive as I would like her to be. Hopefully she'll become more assertive, as she gets older. The last thing I want is for her to be the type of woman that men feel they can disrespect.

Devin is only a year younger than Jayme, and takes after me; she's headstrong and hates to fail at anything. She's going to be successful when she gets older. Right now she has dreams of being in advertising just like her mother. It would break my heart if her dream were to change because of me and my desire for Abe.

Veronica is only four, but is years smarter. She has a mouth so quick and a mind so sharp, she scares me. She has lawyer potential already. She loves her mommy and daddy equally. I try not to imagine what getting caught would do to her.

I knew that crossing the line was dangerous, and there were times when I really thought about putting a stop to it. But the reality is I didn't want to. Whilice and I were growing apart. Our best years were behind us. Sooner or later we were going to break. He may not have known that, but I did.

Damn the consequences.

I picked up the phone and dialed Abe's number. When he didn't answer, I left a message telling him to have sweet dreams. Then I got out of the car.

When I got inside, Whilice and the girls were watching *Madagascar*. They were so wrapped up in it, that all I got was a wave and a smile. I was fine with that. I let my face go, and went into the bedroom to shower and change.

Randy

"What do you mean, you want out?"

I closed my book and stared at Monique, who was standing with her back to me in front of the bedroom window. "What do you mean, Monique?" I asked again.

With a sigh, Monique answered, "I mean I want a break, Randy. I'm moving out."

I got out of bed and approached her. Staring at her reflection in the glass, I said, "Moving out? A break?"

She stared back at me through the glass with seriousness in her eyes, her lips pressed tightly together. She stayed that way for a good half a minute before she responded, and when she did, her tone was all business. "I'm tired of putting up with the bullshit, Randy. That's all there is to it. I'm tired of your inability to be a man."

I stepped away from her and went back to the bed. I sat down and rested my elbows on my knees. "You're not going to start this Tina crap again, are you? We've gone over this song too many times. Do we have to repeat it again?"

"No. I'm tired of the song too."

"So just like that you're going to move out?"

"Yeah. Just like that."

"What about the commitment we made to each other?"

"What about it?"

"Doesn't it mean anything?"

"Yes it does, Randy. It means everything to me. But we made it to each other. Not to each other and Tina."

I exhaled and picked up the book I was reading. I held it tightly in my hands, trying to compose myself and not rip it in half out of frustration. "Please, Monique. Let's be reasonable. What you're saying doesn't make any sense."

"Randy, what I'm saying is true and you know it. Tina is very much a part of this relationship."

Unable to keep myself in check, I threw the book across the room and lay back on the bed. I couldn't believe this was happening. More importantly, I couldn't believe how right she was. Tina was a part of the relationship. But damn it, she was my daughter's mother. "She's Jalisa's mother, Monique. There's only so much I can do about her."

"Whatever, Randy. I really don't care anymore. You can do whatever you want. I want out . . . at least for a while. I just need some time to think. And you need some time to figure out who and what is important to you."

I gritted my teeth and balled my fists tightly, and

wished to God I could have walked out of there and gone to the gym to go a few rounds with the punching bag. I couldn't believe we were having this discussion. I couldn't believe I'd let things get as bad as they had. "What do you want me to do, Monique? Just tell me. I don't want you to leave."

"Randy, if you didn't want me to leave, you would have done something about Tina months ago, instead of avoiding her phone calls—at least when I was around."

"What do you mean by that? I hope you're not insinuating what I think you are."

"What could I possibly be *insinuating*, Randy? All you did was not take her call when I was there. It's not like you did anything different whenever I wasn't around, right?"

"Right."

Monique moved away from the window and walked to the closet, and for the first time I realized she was fully dressed, while I was still in my sweats. "Do you have feelings for her?" she asked, stepping inside and staring at her wardrobe.

"Come on, Monique. You already know the answer to that."

She pulled out a couple of shirts and pants and looked at me. "Do I? Do you?"

My voice was rising in pitch. "What do you mean 'Do I'? You damn well know I don't have any feelings for her."

Monique rolled her eyes and curled her lips. "Just thought I'd ask," she said.

Her flippant attitude was really pissing me off. "Dealing with Tina isn't easy, Monique. You know that. Putting up with her bullshit isn't something I enjoy."

"You may not enjoy it, but you certainly don't put a stop to it, Randy. And you damn sure don't put a stop to her interfering with what we've got going. It's been this way since I first met her. Attitude. That's all I've been putting up with from her. And instead of putting her in check, you ask me to keep my claws in. *Me*! She's Jalisa's mother, which is fine, but just because she is, that doesn't mean she should be able to do or say whatever the hell she wants to, to me.

"Fuck my claws! I refuse to be disrespected, especially in my own home. And I refuse to accept the fact that when I say something to her stupid ass, I'm the only person to whom you have something to say. No, no, no! Not anymore."

I stood up and approached her, but stopped when she put up her hands. "Baby—"

"Enough, Randy! I've had enough. Tina is a bitch. Plain and simple. And that bitch has a problem with the woman you say you love. Now, I know you want to have a relationship with her for Jalisa's sake. I know you want Jalisa to see both parents getting along. I applaud you for wanting that. Kids need that. But you have to accept the reality that you and Tina are not on the same page. She could give two shits about the things you want. What she *wants* is you. What she *wants* is me out of the picture. Being friends with me around is not in her game plan."

I shook my head. "Monique—"

"Randy, there are a lot of parents who don't get

along. There are a lot of kids who have to deal with that. That's real. Sometimes we don't get all of the things we want. I would have thought you would have understood that a long time ago."

"Moniquè, I don't want my little girl growing up in an environment of hostility. Because the minute I tell Tina the deal, that's what she's going to be seeing."

"Jalisa can deal with it."

"I don't want her to have to deal with it."

"Then you don't need me around."

And just like that, she left.

Packed a few things and went to stay with her mother, leaving me with nothing but, "I hope you take the time to figure out what you want."

What I want.

I punched the front door.

Damn.

At that moment, what I wanted was for the clock to be rewound to just before I slept with Tina. I would have used a condom then, instead of believing her when she said she was on the pill. I turned around to see Jalisa stepping out of her bedroom with tears leaking from her eyes.

"Munchkin," I whispered. "Why are you crying?" I walked over to her and picked her up and rocked her tiny body. "What's wrong, little lady?"

She rubbed her eyes and looked at me with red, slightly puffy eyes that broke my heart. "Mommy made Monique go away, didn't she?"

I sighed and squeezed my little princess tightly. Instead of answering her, I just rocked her softly, cursing Tina for being the bitch that she was. I also cursed myself for ever wishing to use a condom.

The next couple of weeks were rough. I tried to call Monique repeatedly on her cell, but she never answered. I called her mother's house, but she never took my calls. I went to her office, but she always refused to see me. Once, I sat in my car all day, parked next to hers, hoping to get her to talk to me, but when she came out of the building to leave, she had security with her.

Eventually, she came and got a few more things. When she did, I tried to talk to her, but all I got was, "I need more time." Then she left again, and I was stuck with nothing but too much time. Three months had now passed and I was losing all hope.

Tina continued to call my cell. I never answered when she did, though, because I just didn't feel like dealing with her. I did let Jalisa call and speak to her though, but I made sure she knew not to mention what had happened. And when Tina asked to speak to me, I had Jalisa tell her that I was busy. It was at those moments that I realized just how much my little girl was growing up. She understood everything that was going on, which made me curse myself even more. I thought about the things Monique had said. That Jalisa could deal with it. I was beginning to see more and more how right she was.

Damn, I missed her. And I wasn't the only one.

"Daddy, is Monique ever going to come back?"

I sipped on my Coke as we sat in the park and watched people roller-blade by. "I don't know, munchkin. She's pretty mad right now."

"At Mommy?"

"At Mommy, and Daddy."

"What did you do?"

"All of the wrong things."

She looked up at me. "Why?"

"I was weak."

"You're not weak, Daddy. You're the strongest daddy in the whole universe. You can pick me up with one arm."

I kissed my little-big woman and she gave me a hug. "You should do the right thing, Daddy. That's what you and Monique always say."

I smiled and kissed my little psychiatrist. "So you think Daddy should be strong?"

"Yup."

I drank down some more of my soda. Jalisa was right. I needed to be strong. It was time. Unfortunately, I lost my strength that night.

It was midnight, and I had just finished doing some work on my laptop, and was getting ready to turn on the TV when my phone rang. Because I had been wishing for it all day, without hesitation, I grabbed at the phone, never even bothering to look at the caller ID.

"Hello?"

"It's about time you answered my call."

Instantly aggravated, I said, "What do you want, Tina?"

"To talk. How's my little girl?"

"She's sleeping. Which is what I'm about to do. Call her back tomorrow night *before* she goes to bed."

"I miss you, Randy."

I breathed out into the phone for her to hear

my frustration. "Tina, don't start, okay. It's late. I'm tired and not in the mood."

As always, she was relentless.

"I bet I could get you in the mood."

"Tina . . ."

"Don't deny it, Randy. You know I could, just like I used to. I still know where your spot is. Does she know where it is?"

"Monique, Tina. And don't mention her again."

"You sound like you need a massage. Why don't you sneak out and come over here and let me rub those strong shoulders?"

"Stop talking shit, Tina. You know I'm not having that. Besides, aren't you in Paris?"

"The shoot ended earlier than expected. I'm back in New York. So you see, if you come over, I could show you how much fun you could be having."

"Jalisa's here, Tina."

"So? Leave her with Monique."

"Monique's not here," I said, grimacing as I instantly regretted letting that slip from my lips.

"It's after twelve and she's not there?" Tina asked in a mischievous tone. "My, my . . . is there trouble in paradise?"

"No trouble."

"Then where is she?"

I was about to snap on her, when the phone beeped, letting me know that I had another call.

Monique?

I looked at the time. It was going on twelve-thirty. Who else could it have been? I looked at the caller ID and sighed.

"I have another call, Tina."

"I'll hold on."

I resisted from cursing her out and clicked over. "Travis?"

"Hey, big brother."

"Hey, little brother. I haven't heard from you in a while."

I listened to my youngest brother sigh, and immediately I knew something was wrong, which didn't surprise me, because he only ever called when something was wrong.

Travis is gay.

Not the in-the-closet or down-low type, but the flamboyantly I'm-flaunting-it-without-shame-for-all-the-world-to-see type. For as long as I could remember, he'd been gay. Growing up, he never liked doing any of the things that "normal" boys liked to do. He preferred Barbie dolls and Easy-Bake ovens over G.I. Joes and He-Man. When he played outside, he hung out with the girls and jumped double Dutch, instead of throwing the football with the guys or playing three-on-three on the basketball court. He liked to decorate sand castles instead of build them.

I won't lie: I was never happy that my youngest brother was gay. Actually, it bothered the hell out of me. Although it wasn't common knowledge, it was obvious to everyone that Travis was a homosexual. Growing up, I used to get into so many fights over comments both guys and girls would make about my brother's sexuality. I was constantly defending what I knew was the truth, and constantly coming to my little brother's aid. It was embarrassing and difficult to deal with, and some days I wished he weren't my brother. But he was, and although it wasn't easy, I learned to accept reality for what it was. My mother did the same, and refused to treat him as anything but her son.

Unfortunately, my father and younger brother, Abe, couldn't deal with the truth, and for years they tried to ignore it, which, I'm sure, they would probably have done all their lives had Travis never come out of the closet during family dinner at sixteen years old. That day changed everything. Until that moment, Travis was my father's son. But right after Travis made his announcement, that all changed.

With the truth now out there and tangible, my father was no longer able to live in the denial he had been living in, and within a matter of seconds after the declaration, my father flew off the handle, and called Travis every demeaning name he could think of. He put him down relentlessly, calling him an embarrassment, a freak, a homo.

"I will not have a homo living in my home! You are not my son!" he screamed.

My younger brother Abraham and I sat silent while our mother yelled and cried for our father to stop with his vicious tirade. All the while, Travis sat stoic in his chair with tears streaming from his eyes, taking everything my father had to offer. Eventually the verbal assault just became too much and he got up from the table and left the house.

Three days passed before he came back home. Our father wasn't home when he did, so my mother took the opportunity to make sure his stomach was full. When he was done eating, he showered, put on fresh clothing, and then came into the bedroom where Abe and I had been sitting silently. He looked at both of us, but didn't say a word. I could see in his eyes that he was looking for approval and support. Not knowing the right thing to say, I remained silent, and instead gave him a reassuring nod. Obviously, I would have preferred that he not be gay, but I'd come to grips with the fact that he was a long time ago, so I couldn't turn my back on him, and that's what I told him with my nod.

I'll never forget the smile of appreciation he gave to me right before Abe, who hadn't said a word about Travis's coming out since the dinner, finally reacted. There was so much happiness in that smile. In that moment, he seemed at ease. But that was only for a fleeting second, because before I even realized it was happening, Abe jumped up from his bed and gave Travis a vicious blow to the face, breaking his nose instantly. Older by six years, Abe knocked Travis down and pummeled him with numerous hate-filled left and right body blows until I wrestled him off. Abe tried to go at it with me, but, before he could connect, I wrapped him up in a bear hug and pinned him to the ground.

Unable to break free from my grasp, he stopped fighting and just stared at our younger brother, and in a very quiet, yet lethal voice said, "Don't ever speak to me again, you motherfucking faggot. You're not my fucking brother."

Forcing his way out of my grasp, Abe got up from the floor and left the room, and left me alone to help my bloodied brother to the bathroom to clean his wounds. Abe never spoke to Travis again, while I've been helping to clean up his wounds ever since.

My brother's lifestyle isn't the greatest and on one too many occasions, I've had to rescue him from ugly situations. Like I said, he's really flamboyant and he doesn't seem to understand that not everyone is willing to tolerate his boisterous ways. He's been in and out of the hospital more times than I care to remember, because of being beaten up not only by pissed-off heterosexuals, but by the abusive boyfriends he's had as well. Sometimes I couldn't help but wonder if he was trying to commit suicide by living the way he did.

"What happened now, Travis?"

He sighed again and then very quietly said, "I need a favor."

"What's new? What do you need?"

"I need you to come and get me out of the hospital tomorrow."

"You're in there again?" I shook my head. "What happened this time?"

"I . . . had a fight with Paul."

"You're still with that guy? I thought you would have learned your lesson after the last three times."

"Paul's not bad, Randy. He has a very stressful job. Sometimes it's just too much for him and he has to vent."

"How long are you going to let him take his frustrations out on you, Travis?"

"Look, Randy, please spare me the sermon. I don't need to hear it right now. Are you gonna pick me up tomorrow or not?"

"Whatever, man. Your funeral. Where are you, and what time?"

After getting the information from Travis, I

hung up the phone, forgetting that Tina had still been on hold. The phone rang, reminding me. I reluctantly picked it up.

"Sorry about that," I said, unable to hide my frustration.

"Baby, what's wrong? I can hear in your voice that was a bad call."

"That was my brother."

"He still living like there's no tomorrow?"

"Only way he knows how."

Tina smacked her lips. She never cared for Travis. "Oh well," she said. "When you choose to live in sin like that—"

"Cut it, Tina."

Tina smacked her lips again. "Fine. Where did you say Monique was again?"

I squeezed my temples and clenched my jaws. "Tina, I need to get some rest. If you want to talk to Jalisa tomorrow, call at an earlier time."

"Why are you avoiding the question, Randy?" Tina pressed.

"Call Jalisa tomorrow," I said, ignoring her. Before I hung up, I think I heard her say something about coming over. I hoped I was wrong.

Monique

Jazz whispered softly from my speakers as I sat in darkness alone with my thoughts. I was trying to get some work done. Lord knows I needed to, because ever since I left Randy, I hadn't been able to focus and it began to show. I'd lost another case, and I was on the verge of losing another, and as bad as it is to say, I just didn't really care.

I was miserable.

I had never fallen so hard for someone before, the way I had for Randy. He made me feel things that I thought were only possible on the movie screen or in between the pages of romance novels. No matter what I did or didn't do, I couldn't get him off my mind. I missed his smile and his gentle touch. I missed his annoying snoring and the nightly battles for ownership over the blanket. I longed for his good-bye hugs and hello kisses. My days just didn't begin or end the same without them. I never realized how big a role he played in my life until he was no longer by my side.

But it wasn't just his habits and the comfort of knowing that he was there that I ached for. I had also become extremely close to Jalisa, and to not see her left me with an empty feeling inside that was different from the vacancy I felt over Randy. Without intending on it happening, I had become a mother. Jalisa and I bonded in a way she and Tina never would. It was me that she reached out for when she needed help, and it was me that she looked for when she wanted some attention. I missed not being there for her. Even more so, I missed her not being there for me, as her presence in my life was something that I had come to rely on. Just knowing that with each passing day, I was possibly losing the connection I had with her, made everything that much more frustrating.

The CD changed and switched to an old Color Me Badd disc. It was set on random, and immediately started playing a song that went straight to my heart.

Thinking back.

I listened to the words in the song and thought about how everything used to be for Randy, Jalisa, and me. I thought about all of the moments the three of us spent together. Special nights in front of the television with popcorn, soda, and juice, watching Disney movies. Walking hand-in-hand through the park on sunny days. Despite Tina's best effort at sabotage, nothing had kept us from becoming a family.

I wiped a tear away from the corner of my eye. I was lonely without them. Lonely and angry. The more I thought about the whole situation and the way it affected everything, the angrier I became. I felt cheated. Cheated out of love. Cheated out of a family. Cheated out of happiness.

Why the hell couldn't Randy have just shut Tina up once and for all? Why did he have to be so damn nonconfrontational? Hell, a little fight every now and then was good for the soul, and after dealing with all of Tina's antics, his soul needed a good cleaning out. I damn sure enjoyed my purification after I hit her.

Thinking about that moment brought a tiny smile to my face. I had needed that release. After Randy and I argued about my having lashed out in front of Jalisa, I felt really guilty. But the more I thought about what I had done and the timing of it all, the more I realized Randy had been trying to protect her from too much. Jalisa was so much older than the five years she'd lived. Whether Randy wanted to accept it or not, she understood what kind of woman her mother was and wasn't. Trying to shield her from a reality she'd long accepted was pointless. But that was one of the things that I loved and hated about him at the same time. He wanted so much for his little girl to have what too many minority children these days didn't have—both parents involved in her life.

Both he and I were fortunate enough to have been raised in a two-parent household. I didn't realize it until I got older, but having both parents really helped mold me into the woman I'd become. I honestly admired what he was trying to do for Jalisa, but some battles, as valiant as they were, just weren't worth the time and effort. Tina was not the woman that our mothers were, and she never would be. I know he knew that. I just wish he would have accepted it. When it came to Tina, I wish he wouldn't have been such a good man.

Randy

After I hung up the phone with Tina, I lay back on the bed and closed my eyes. My head was hurting from all of the frustration.

Frustration over Travis.

Frustration over my father and Abe's relationship with Travis.

Frustration over Tina.

Frustration over what had happened with Monique.

I fell asleep with nothing but frustration running rampant in my mind. Had the doorbell not rung and woken me up, I would have remained sleeping until the sun rose. I lifted my head and looked at the clock and saw that it was almost two in the morning.

Who the hell could it have been at that hour? Again my thoughts went to Monique. And again I was sorely disappointed when I looked through the peephole and saw Tina standing in the hallway.

Shit.

I hadn't been hearing things.

I opened the door.

"What are you doing here?"

"I'm here to give you that massage." She walked past me, with a small bag in hand.

"Tina, you need to leave."

"Why? Monique's not here. If she were, she would have answered the door."

"Tina, you have to leave. Now."

"So what happened with you and the yellow bitch, anyway? Did you finally come to your senses and realize you'd been wasting time with her all along?"

"Tina—"

"You know I'm right, Randy," she said, sashaying toward me. "I can give you everything you want and need. I have money, I have fame. Baby, I know what you like. Monique can't do everything like I can."

As she came forward, I backpedaled slowly until my heel ran into the front of my couch, causing me to fall back into the cushions.

"Why are you fighting the truth, Randy?" Tina asked, licking her lips seductively. She kneeled down in front of me and wrapped her arms around me. "You know how well we work together. How well we fit." She put her hand over my crotch and despite my best effort to keep it from happening, massaged my manhood to life. Damn, if she didn't always have good hands.

"Jalisa's asleep in her bedroom, Tina," I said as goose bumps rose from my skin.

Tina flashed a wicked smile. "I can be quiet, Randy. Can you?"

"You need to go," I tried again.

"I can take good care of you, Randy," she whispered.

"I'm already taken care of," I said, trying to find the willpower to remain strong. Of course, Tina knew I was losing the battle.

She put her fingers to my lips. "Shhh. Let me show you how good it is. Let me give it to you like you remember it."

Suddenly her lips were on mine, and as much as my mind told me to, I didn't pull back. I just opened my mouth and allowed her tongue to dance with my own. I can't lie; I had been horny as hell since Monique had gone. Allowing what was happening to happen was wrong, but shit, I was tired of masturbating to adult movies on Showtime.

I drove my tongue further into Tina's mouth, and slipped my hand under her sweatshirt and grabbed her breast that hadn't been confined by a bra. She moaned softly, making my manhood even harder, as I squeezed her nipples in a not-so-gentle manner. With no complaint from her, I lifted the sweatshirt and took her mounds into my mouth and ran my tongue over and around her nipples as if they had been coated with my favorite—strawberry jelly.

Tina moaned, unbuttoned my shirt halfway, ran her hand over my chest, and then undid my belt, unbuckled my jeans, and slid her hand beneath my boxers. I got chills and almost couldn't catch my breath as she stroked me slowly, expertly. Without words, she had me stand, and when I did, she slid my pants and boxers down to my ankles, and then took me into her mouth. I had to focus damn hard to keep myself from exploding as her tongue ran along my shaft and then rolled around the tip of my penis.

Damn hard.

Tina looked up at me and smiled as her mouth and hand worked in unison. I wanted to, but I couldn't look away. I was her prisoner and my release wouldn't come until I released. Goddamn, she wasn't lying when she said she knew how to put it on me. But then so did Monique.

Shit.

Monique.

"Stop!"

Tina looked up at me with my penis in her mouth and mumbled, "Excuse me?"

I reclaimed ownership of my quickly softening member and shook my head. I couldn't believe that I'd gone there with her.

Damn.

I pulled up my boxers and zipped up my pants.

Tina's face was plastered with a look of complete and utter shock, and was getting uglier by the second. "What the hell is this all about?" she snapped.

"Tina, you have to go."

"Go? What do you mean, go? How could you say that after what just happened?"

"What just happened was a mistake. A slip in judgement."

"A slip—" She stood up and tried to take my hand in hers, but I wouldn't allow it. "How could you say that was a mistake? What just happened was real. You know that."

"Tina, you have to go," I said again. "This wasn't supposed to happen, and it's not going to happen."

Tina placed a hand on her hip, pulled her neck back a bit and stuck an index finger at me. "You think you can treat me like some two-dollar ho, get your dick sucked and then tell me to leave? I don't fucking think so!"

"You know that's not how it went down. Stop tripping, and keep your voice down. Jalisa's sleeping."

"Stop tripping?" she said, ignoring my request. "Nigga, the only one tripping here is your ass."

"That's right, Tina, I'm tripping. Now grab your shit and get the fuck out." I was burning inside; pissed at myself for what I let happen.

Tina and I stared at one another for a few seconds. I was sure she was going to explode with another outburst, because rarely had I ever gone off on her like that. To my surprise, though, she chuckled a little, then grabbed her bag and stepped toward me. For a moment I thought she was going to take a swing at me with that bag, but instead, she stopped with her face inches from mine and said, "You know what, Randy? I'm not gonna *trip* anymore, because I know that you'll have me back for more. My shit is good—too good. You can only resist it for so long, and you know it. I can wait while you get your mind right."

"My mind is just fine."

"We'll see."

She kissed me on my mouth and then stepped past me. I wiped my lips and followed behind her, tempted to kick her in her ass to make her leave faster. Before I opened the door, she turned around and smiled at me. "Give *our* little girl a kiss good night for me."

I resisted the urge to say anything and just opened the door. When I did, my jaw slacked, and my mouth fell to the ground.

In the doorway stood Monique.

Tina turned around and gave me an evil smile. "Well, I can see I'm no longer needed here. Don't hesitate to call me again, Randy." She walked past Monique, and as she did, she waved. "Damn, I need to go home and shower," she sang, walking down the hall.

In front of me, Monique stood silent, stoic. She held the house key that she'd never returned in her hand. Damn.

"Baby, I can explain. It's not what it looks like." But it was. As I stood there with my shirt unbuttoned and my pants unbuckled, it was exactly what it seemed to be. I kept trying, though. "Baby, I'm so glad to see you."

She looked down to my unbuckled pants and then back up at me. "I guess you were glad to see Tina too."

"Monique, it's not what—"

"Spare me the explanation, you ass. I came because I missed you and wanted to work everything out. But I see you've already moved on."

"Monique, I didn't invite Tina over. She just showed up."

"And you did your best to get her to leave."

"Nothing happened. I swear."

Monique looked down at my unbuckled pants again. "Nothing hap—you know what? I don't need this."

"Nothing happened," I said again.

"I don't give a shit if anything did or not, Randy!" she yelled. "Here." She grabbed my hand and slammed the house key into my palm. "I don't want any damn explanations. It's past two o'clock in the fucking morning, Tina just left, and you're standing in front of me with your shirt unbuttoned and your pants undone. I think most people call that a booty call. Good-bye, Randy. Don't fucking call me anymore. Don't try to come see me anymore. As a matter of fact, don't even think about me. Just do me one favor."

"Monique . . . please . . ."

"Tell Jalisa I said good-bye."

Without another word, she turned and walked away. I called out to her, but she never stopped. I wanted to run after her, but decided not to. The damage was already done. I fucked up, and now I had been left with nothing but an abandoned key and my shame.

Abe

Nakyia and I were chilling on South Beach when I faintly heard my cell phone vibrating in my bag. I looked at Nakyia to see if she had noticed it, but she hadn't. She was having one of her good days when the pain wasn't too severe. She said she wanted to go to the beach, soak in some fresh air, and let the sounds of the ocean massage her mind. I didn't mind that at all. Beaches were always good for the mind, body, soul.

I loved South Beach in June. Thongs, string bikinis; what more could a man ask for? I discreetly reached into my bag and pressed a button to stop my cell's vibration, and then lay back on the towel with my shades on and did some subtle sightseeing while my wife read the latest novel by one of her favorite authors, Roy Glenn.

"Don't be afraid to leave me here and go in the water," Nakyia said, looking up from her book. "I know how you love the sea."

"I'm cool right here with you, ladylove. Besides,

I'm not in the mood to swim today anyway. Too tired."

Which I was, because I'd been with Taki the night before. I'd told Nakyia I had to work late, and then I was going to go out with my boy, Jeff, who wasn't really my boy. He just worked in the finance department downstairs. He was the only one who knew about the relationship Taki and I had. He'd been in his car one night about to leave, when he saw us kissing each other good-bye. Taki's back was to him, so she had no idea he'd been there.

"What's up, Jeff?" As soon as Taki had driven away, I approached his car.

He turned the key in the ignition. "Chillin'." Silence passed between us for a hot minute, before he said, "Yo, I didn't see a thing."

"You sure?" I asked skeptically.

"I'm sure. Just like you're sure you didn't see anything when I was saying good-bye to Lisa a couple of months ago."

I gave him a nod and pound, and that was the end of that. As long as I had his back, he would have mine.

I took a small break from my sightseeing and looked up at the clouds in the clear-blue sky. It really was a beautiful day. I was glad Nakyia suggested we get out. It felt good being there with her. It was nice seeing her in a cheerful and bright mood. She used to be a very affectionate woman, which is one of the things I loved most about her. But after the neuralgia, all that stopped. I looked away from the sky and watched her read her book. She was actually smiling without grimacing, and that gave me a pleasant chill. I missed her carefree smile. It was something I rarely got to see. For a brief moment, I was jealous of Mr. Glenn for accomplishing a feat I couldn't seem to do, no matter how hard I tried sometimes.

"Good book?" I asked.

"Mmm-hmm," she said with another smile. "Roy Glenn's characters know the time when it comes to dealing with someone that's betrayed their trust. One bullet to the brain. What better message is there?"

She was looking dead at me when she said that, and I don't know why, but I swear it felt like she'd been giving me a message of her own. I shrugged off the feeling, though, rationalizing that my conscience had been fucking with me.

I gave her a smile and then went back to my sightseeing. A few minutes later, as I started to doze off to the sounds of the waves hitting the shore and the seagulls in the air, my cell phone vibrated again. I took a quick look over at Nakyia. She'd fallen asleep with her book lying across her chest. I waited for a moment to see if she'd notice the vibration, and when she didn't stir, I reached into my bag, grabbed my phone, and took a quick look to see who was calling. When I saw who it was, I slid the phone into my pocket, and stood up. As I did, Nakyia opened her eyes. She started to speak, but before she could, another jolt of pain came on. I watched helplessly as her face twisted, and her mouth hung open. I hated seeing that. I hated that I couldn't take the pain away. When the pain finally subsided, she composed herself and said, "Couldn't stay away from the water, huh?"

I knelt down and kissed her on her forehead. "Yeah, but I'm not gonna swim, though. I just want to feel the water on my feet. Then I may take a walk over to one of the shops for a bite to eat. You want to come?" I asked, already knowing what her answer was going to be.

Nakyia shook her head. "No. My nerve is starting to act up. It's about time for me to take my medicine. You go ahead."

I kissed her forehead again and stood up. "Okay, sexy. I won't be too long."

I strolled down to the water just like I said I would, and then headed off the sand to Ocean Drive. I nearly tripped a couple of times, as I passed by honeys of all shapes, colors, and sizes. When it came to fine ass, South Beach had more than enough. Being married could be a cruel punishment sometimes.

When I got away from the beach and the distractions, at least the ones in the thongs on the sand, I grabbed my phone and returned Taki's call. "You called?"

Her voice was honey when she spoke. "Yes I did, handsome. Did you listen to the voice mail I left you?"

"No."

"I want to see you. Whilice took the kids to a movie, and then they're going to visit his parents. I told him I had some work to do, so I'm free all day."

I smiled as a Latina with a body full of seduction walked past me and gave me the up-and-down. I had to turn around when she passed me and admire her sashay. "Abe?" I heard Taki say.

Another cutie with skin the color of dark chocolate walked past me, and after we traded admiring glances, I put my focus back on the call.

"I can't today, Taki. I'm spending the day with Nakyia. We're at the beach right now."

She sighed into the phone, and sucked her teeth. "I want to see you bad, baby. I'm wet just thinking about what I want to do to you here on my water bed."

I looked at the waves in the ocean and imagined swelling up and down on that bed with Taki above me naked and sweating. I felt myself harden, which wasn't cool because I didn't have my shirt on to hide behind. I turned away from the ocean view, and focused on a pile of garbage; I needed something ugly to change the thoughts in my mind. But Taki wasn't trying to let me off the hook.

"I bought a new massaging oil that I want to put to use. It gets hot with friction."

"Taki, you need to chill. I can't today. Teasing me won't do you or myself any good."

"Mmmm, baby. If you could see me now. . . ."

Damn.

I slid my hand into my pocket and, very discreetly, adjusted myself, trying my best to keep anyone from noticing the hard-on I was getting.

Damn, she knew how to work me. I looked at the rise and fall of the ocean again. I wanted to be there with Nakyia, but the thought of being inside of Taki was almost too much. I still tried to resist, though. "Taki, I really wish I could, but I promised Nakyia we would spend today together. Besides, we need to chill and keep it discreet. Being in your crib is not being discreet."

"But it would be fun," Taki purred.

"Yeah, maybe. But unless you could guarantee that Whilice wouldn't show up, there's no chance of that happening."

"Abe," she whispered. I could tell that she was getting off on the phone.

A brother could only adjust himself but so much. I had to end the call, but the sound of her voice and the image I had in my mind made it damn near impossible. More honeys walked by; I wondered if any of them noticed the bulge.

"Abe," she whispered again. "Meet me in the office if you don't want to be here. I'll bring the oil. I want to show you how warm it gets."

Shit.

I was sweating.

And it wasn't from the heat.

"All right. Give me a few. I'll call you when I'm ready."

"Hurry baby. The cat is purring and wants some milk."

I hung up before she could say another word. I crossed the street and stood outside the gates of where Versace was killed. I had a couple of Versace suits at home. Damn shame he was gone. I moved from there and walked past patrons sitting outside of a bar enjoying beer and food, under the shade of umbrellas. I needed a cold one myself.

I crossed back to the beach and stepped onto the hot sand. I was burning inside. Taki had me on fire. I figured there was no better excuse than work.

"Baby," I said, tapping Nakyia gently. She'd fallen asleep again. I sighed. She looked so peaceful with the book lying beside her. This was the only time she truly got relief from the neuralgia. How could I disturb that? I shook my head, disgusted by what I was going to do, and decided to call Taki and tell her that I wasn't going to be able to meet her.

As I stood up to walk away, Nakyia opened her eyes. "Hey handsome. What do . . ." she paused as another wave of pain came over her. "What . . . do you need?" she finished, when it subsided.

I looked at her and cursed myself. This was supposed to be our day. I'd promised it to her. We needed days like this.

"Abe? What's . . . what's wrong?"

I continued to look at her, but didn't speak. At that moment my big head was battling my little head.

My wife or Taki.

My wife, who couldn't let loose, or Taki, who wanted to do just that and more.

"Abe?" Nakyia said, grabbing my attention.

I clenched my jaws and looked out to the waves rising in the ocean. Rising like Taki would on top of me in the office where she was waiting for me. "I'm sorry to do this," I said, feeling like such a bastard. "But my boss just called. She and the VP are having a big meeting tomorrow, and she needs some information that I have. The only problem is the things I need are at work."

Nakyia frowned, only adding to the guilt and shame I felt. "Do you have to go? There's no way you can get this done in the morning?"

"Unfortunately, no. I have too much going on in the morning to spend time on this. Believe me, I'm just as upset about this as you are. I even told her that I was at the beach."

"And?"

"And she wasn't trying to hear it. She wants the info today."

"What a bitch."

"You can say that again."

She did.

I shrugged my shoulders and said, "Unfortunately, I need the job."

Nakyia sat up, took my hand in hers, and placed it on her left cheek. The right side of her face was always off-limits. "We better get going then."

I looked at her and frowned. *Why did she have to be so damn understanding?* "I'll make this up to you. I promise."

She smiled and said, "I'm sure you will."

We left the beach, and headed back to West Kendall, where we live in the Villas of Barcelona. It's a gated community that gives an impression of an old world village. Our villa is Mediterranean-style with three bedrooms, and warm sun-and earth-colored walls and a Spanish-style tiled roof. It's reminiscent of the beauty of Barcelona. The community itself has a recreation center with a wet bar, gymnasium, whirlpool, and swimming pool. It's almost like living in an old, Spanish city. At least that's what the brochure said. Nakyia chose it. She liked the Spanish flair, and she also liked the fact that it was peaceful and clean. I had no problem with her choice, because after the first visit, I saw that we would have some fine honeys for neighbors.

When we got home, because the medicine she'd taken had kicked in, Nakyia went straight to the bed to lie down. I made her a cup of tea, and turned on some light jazz for her to sleep to. After that I jumped in the shower. When I finished getting ready, I knelt beside the bed and placed a very gentle, yet careful kiss on Nakyia's lips. I loved my wife very much, and for a brief moment, I was tempted to undress, cuddle in the bed beside her, and forget all about Taki and her massage oil. But my penis wasn't having it; just the mere thought of the oil made it jump. It was time to go.

I changed the CD collection in the player, and left while Howard Hewett sang about how much he loved his lady. In the car, I called Taki and told her I was on the way.

Monique

"I can't believe he had the nerve to have that bitch there!"

I continued to squeeze the hell out of my stress ball as I paced a hole in my mother's beige carpeting. I'd just finished recounting the episode with Randy to her, and as direct as only she could be, she expressed how unsurprised she was to hear the news.

"Randy's a man, Monique. That's what they do. When they can't have one woman, they always go running for the closest one they can find. It's in their nature to think with their little head and not the big one."

"I thought Randy was different," I said with a sigh.

"Like I said, he's a man. Be glad that you caught him red-handed."

"Well, I wouldn't exactly call it red-handed."

"Monique, his pants were unbuckled, his shirt was damn near hanging off his shoulders, and that bitch was just leaving his place talking about how she needed a shower. If that's not red-handed I don't know what is."

"Tina probably said that just to get under my skin."

My mother sucked her teeth. "Unbuckled pants. Unbuttoned shirt. Tina being there in the middle of the night while you weren't there. Need I go on?"

I wanted to say something in defense of Randy again, although I don't know why, but couldn't think of anything to counter my mother's break-down. She was right: Tina's comment didn't really matter. I may not have had hard evidence, but the evidence I did have was good enough.

My mother mmm-hmm'd and gave me a you-know-I'm-right look. "Now you can stop wasting your time, baby, and find a man that's worthy of you. I know it's not an easy thing to accept, but the fact is, Randy just isn't as different as you thought he was. I think you need to admit to yourself that he may in fact be a housebroken dog, who never quite got the hang of not digging in the trash for snacks. I think—"

"Mom, I really don't want to hear anymore, okay? I don't mean to be rude, but let's face it . . . you're not going to win any citizenship awards for being nice to men."

My mother sucked her teeth again. "Baby, as soon as men do something to earn my pleas-antries, I'll change. But until then, they are out of luck."

"You know you're only like that because of Dad."

"Baby girl, don't you mention your father in this house, please."

"Mom, not all men are like Dad. Not all men run around sleeping with any women they can, or sleeping with their wive's best friends."

"No, baby, you're right. Not all men are filthy dogs like your father. Not all men go tramping around. But apparently Randy seems to be one of those men."

I deformed my stress ball again as I thought about my mother's last comment. I really thought Randy was different. That he was incapable of falling into the pit of the trifling. But like my mom had said, how much more proof had I needed?

I paced, exhaled, and squeezed. Paced, exhaled, and squeezed. The more pacing I did, the more squeezing I did. The more squeezing I did, the angrier I became as pictures flashed in my mind.

Randy and Tina.

Tina smiling in my face as she walked past me.

Tina's comment about needing a shower.

Randy with his pants unbuckled, his zipper partly down, his shirt unbuttoned.

Randy with the look of guilt written all over his face.

Paced, exhaled, and squeezed. Paced, exhaled, and squeezed.

I wanted to replace the stress ball with Randy and Tina's necks, and wring them both until their eyes bulged out. Why did he have to hurt me like that? I knew he was incapable of putting Tina in her place, but actually sleeping with her? What's worse, Jalisa was there.

Paced, exhaled and squeezed. Paced, exhaled and squeezed.

I paced until my fingers got stiff, and my legs told me that it was time to sit my ass down. When I did, I grabbed my cell phone and turned it on. I'd turned it off after the thousandth time Randy had called me. It beeped, letting me know that I had a voice mail message. After the last two hundred he'd left, I had no doubt that it was another one from Randy.

Begging for a chance to explain.

Trying to convince me that he and Tina hadn't done anything.

Insisting that it was all a misunderstanding.

I took a deep breath and rubbed my temples. What if they hadn't done anything? What if I had misunderstood what I'd walked in on? Maybe I should hear him out. Maybe I should let him explain. I took another deep breath and squeezed my eyes tightly, trying to keep tears from falling.

What if?

I looked at my cell phone, contemplated *what if* again, and passed my fingers over the keypad.

What if?

But it was past two in the morning, and if a woman is leaving a man's place, and his clothing was in the condition like Randy's, there's only one thing they could have been doing.

The nerve of him to tell me that he loved me.

Tina. I hate that bitch. I hate that Randy let her come in between what we had. It wasn't fair. Why the hell couldn't he have been man enough to put a stop to her? I mean, if he loved me the way he said he did, wouldn't he have done that?

"Don't hesitate to call me again, Randy."
Bitch.
I pressed the button to delete all messages, cursed Randy out in my mind, let the tears that I just couldn't hold back any longer, fall, and asked myself one question: why the hell did I still love him?

Abe

From the moment I stepped into Taki's office, it was on.

It was a humid eighty-five-degree evening, and she was wearing a long trench coat, closed only by the belt around her waist. My mind instantly thought of the scene where Robin Givens walked into Eddie Murphy's crib and showed him what she hadn't been wearing in the movie *Boomerang*. Taki did the same for me. Just like Robin, underneath she wore nothing but an outfit that was straight out of a Frederick's of Hollywood catalogue—a red satin-and-lace garter belt with lace stockings accentuating her athletic legs. Only partly covering her breasts was a matching lace bra, which had slits in the middle to expose her nipples.

I had just enough time to admire her and say, "Mmm-mmm-mmm," before the coat she'd been holding open was dropped to the ground and she jumped into my arms.

I cradled her breasts and slid my tongue right in between the slits, running them over her hard nipples. She moaned in appreciation as I did so, and when I moved from her breasts to her neck, she ran her hands over my bald dome, and then slid her hands under my shirt and ran them around the base of my waist, which she knew drove me insane. Before I knew it, my pants had been unbuckled, unzipped, and my penis went smoothly from her hands to her mouth, and was worked to its fullest extent. As she stroked me, she applied some of the massage oil she'd been so determined to use. With each caress the oil grew hotter, and so did I as I pulsated and gyrated to the rhythm her hands and mouth created.

Without missing a beat, she dimmed her halogen lamp, and eased me down to the floor, where I sat with my back against the wall. I was pleasantly surprised when she straddled me and slid me inside of her without removing her panties, which were crotchless.

She was so moist that I was momentarily paralyzed. While she rode me with the fierce expertise of a bull rider, she cupped my chin with one hand, forcing me to look up at her, and grabbed her breast with the other and lifted it towards her tongue. I watched her intensely as she worked magic with her pussy and tongue at the same time. My concentration was broken for a brief moment when a photo of her husband and kids caught my eye, but I rectified that by taking my foot and kicking her desk, causing it to fall facedown.

"What's wrong?" she asked in mid-stride.

"Nothing. I just had to get rid of a cramp."

We went at it until we were both spent and satisfied, after which we sat on the floor, her head resting on my shoulder, and her legs wrapped around mine. Everything was tight—her lingerie, the oil, and the way she rode; I just knew I was going to sleep well that night.

But then she started talking.

My eyes were closed and my body was relaxed as I waited for my manhood to recover and be ready to go another round, when out of the blue she asked the question that she was never supposed to ask.

"Abe, where are we going with this?"

I had a feeling this was going to happen, though. I prayed it wouldn't, but I just couldn't shake the feeling that it would. I saw it in her eyes more and more; I felt it with every departing hug.

I opened my eyes. "What do you mean, where are we going?"

She lifted her head and looked at me. "I mean, where are we taking this relationship?"

Relationship?

"What do you mean by *relationship*, Taki? We're both married."

"I know. And we're both unhappy."

"I'm not unhappy."

"Then why have you been seeing me?"

I was frustrated and didn't want to have the conversation. I shrugged her off of me and stood up. Immediately my mind flashed back to Michael Douglas. Damn. I had to use tact. I exhaled and reached for my boxers. Recovered or not, my dick was done for the night. Or at least I was.

"Taki," I said sliding them on, and doing my best to keep my voice calm. "We both knew that we could only take this but so far. It's always been a physical thing. I don't know how unhappy you are or aren't, but I'm not unhappy with Nakyia. There are just some things that she's not able to do for me, that you can. I thought you understood that?"

Taki stayed on the ground, brought her knees to her chest, and cradled them with her arms. I went about gathering the rest of my clothing and angrily bit down on my lip. All we ever did was fuck. We never cuddled—at least not in the realest sense of the word. Our kisses were passionate, but never filled with romance. We fucked. We never made love, and never let it get any further than that.

I should have known better than to think a woman, however down with the situation she claimed to be, was going to be able to handle that type of relationship without her emotions coming into play.

"I do understand, Abe," Taki said. "It's just that . . . well, I have developed feelings . . . deep feelings for you. I didn't plan on it happening. It just did. You're special to me, and I . . . I think I'm fall— well, don't you have any feelings for me at all? Or am I just a fuck buddy to keep you occupied?"

I wanted to answer that question as honestly as I could, but again, with the predicament I was in, I had to answer this correctly. Like I said before, I didn't need the Demi Moore shit in my life. Damn it, why did I have to go and fuck around with my boss?

"No," I said, continuing to get dressed. "I mean, yes, I have feelings for you. And no, you aren't just a fuck buddy. I like you, Taki. I really do. But I have to be honest with you. I'm not in love with you. I'm in love with my wife."

There was silence for a good three minutes, and in that time, I finished getting dressed. Taki never moved. She just sat quiet with a blank expression on her face. I couldn't tell whether she was about to cry or blow up, and to tell the truth, I didn't really want to know. I just wanted to get the fuck out of there as fast as I could. But damn it, if I didn't have to come in and deal with her in the morning. I knew I couldn't leave without having everything settled.

I picked up her bra and trench coat. "Are you all right?" I asked, holding them out for her.

Taki stood up and took her bra from my hand. "I'm fine," she snapped.

I took a subtle step back. "I don't want there to be any misunderstanding between us, Taki. If you can't handle this anymore, let me know. I want you to be comfortable. You're important to me," I lied. "I don't want you getting hurt in any way." *Because I need my fucking job,* I would have liked to have added, but kept that thought to myself.

"I said I was fine, Abe," Taki growled. "I'm sorry that everything didn't go according to how you planned it. I'm sorry that I care for you more than you do for me."

"Taki . . ."

"Don't worry, Abe. I won't rock the boat for you and your wife. We did what we came to do. We fucked. Now you can leave."

"Taki . . ." I said again, not feeling comfortable at all with the growing venom in her tone.

"I said I'm fine with the arrangement we have, Abe. No strings attached. No expectations."

I nodded. There really was no point in saying anything else. "Okay, good."

Taki rolled her eyes. "Yeah, it's all good."

We looked at one another for a few seconds and then before anything unpleasant could happen, I turned and left.

Taki

"**S**on of a bitch!"

I slammed my hand down on my steering wheel. "That no-good-want-his-cake-and-eat-it-too son of a bitch!" I slammed the wheel again and pressed down on the gas pedal angrily.

After Abe left, I did the only thing I could do—I cried. I felt like a fool. I'd practically poured my heart out to him and all he could say was that he didn't want any misunderstandings. He didn't even have the decency to give me a hug before he left.

Coward.

I cried until I had no more tears left and then changed into clothes I'd had in a bag in the backseat of my car, and then headed for the expressway. I cruised aimlessly at seventy-five miles an hour, with no specific destination in mind. Going home at that moment wasn't an option, because I knew there was no way I was going to be able to wear my other face for Whilice and the kids.

I slammed my hand down on the steering wheel again. As much as I wanted to put it all on Abe's shoulders, I knew I really had only myself to blame. I let my heart get involved. In reality, Abe's callousness should never have hurt me. I guess deep down I was hoping for a different type of response from him, but I should have known better. After all, we'd both had an understanding from the very beginning. We were just satisfying each other's sexual urge. Plain and simple. There was nothing more to it than that.

I turned on the radio to drown out the noise from inside of my head. Luther Vandross was singing "Always and Forever." How about never and nevermore? I thought.

I got rid of Luther and put it on a Latin station. I didn't know a lick of Spanish, so they could sing about always and forever all they wanted to. But of course with the way my night had been going, I had to hear the one word I did know: *Amor.* Love.

I cursed and turned the radio off.

I thought about what Abe had said: that I did things for him his wife couldn't. I knew about her condition. He had mentioned it to me one day over a casual lunch. We were just coworkers then, although I was drawn to him. I remember feeling so sad for him. The recount of the helplessness he'd expressed pulled at my heartstrings. I found myself wanting to comfort him and make him feel better, which is what I tried to do whenever we were together. I tried to make him forget all about his hardship, and concentrate on our moment. I wanted his thoughts to be focused on my body, my sex, my remedy. Obviously the attention lasted only as long as his dick did.

A car horn suddenly went off and woke me from

my introspection. I had drifted into another lane. I quickly veered back into my lane, and when an elderly man pulled beside me and blew his horn again, I did the only thing I could: I gave him the finger. He looked like he was about to have a heart attack as I sped off. I slammed my wheel once again and cursed him and everyone else.

A half hour passed before I finally looked at the time on the dash. It was nearing eleven P.M. As much as I didn't want to, I had to get home and keep that part of my life in order, while the rest of it tumbled into a state of confusion, because that's just what was happening. I know I'd told Abe that I could deal with things staying the way they were, but I wasn't so sure about that. I was his boss. I was having an affair with him, and I was falling in love. What's worse, I had stripped myself naked and bared my emotions and that meant that I no longer had the control that I so desperately needed anymore. How was I going to be able to continue to work with him? He would never say or show it, but I know he'd lost respect for me.

When I got home, Whilice and the girls were sleeping, so I took advantage of the quiet time and took a bath to try and relax myself and my brain. I lay in the hot water and caressed myself with the Calgon bubbles. For the first time since my conversation with Abe, I was starting to feel the pressure lighten. As my luck would have it, twenty minutes into my escape, the bathroom door creaked open and Whilice appeared in the door jamb wearing nothing but his silk boxers. His bulge of comfort hung just over his waistline and disgusted me. I remember when he used to care about his physique. I used to get jealous from the stares women used to give him. Notice the amount of *used to's?* After he and I said our I do's, everything changed. He let the washboard stomach go, he allowed his muscle to turn into flab, and not even my constant complaining made him change. As far as he was concerned, he was married; he had no one to impress.

He stepped into the bathroom, closed the door, and from behind his back, he presented a bouquet of roses.

Not now.

"What are those for?" I asked, not even attempting to put my mask on.

He sat on the rim of the tub and kissed me on my cheek. "I got your message. The kids and I came home early. I was hoping to spend some time with you. Maybe take you out for some dinner."

"I have a big presentation tomorrow, so I had to go to the office and get some things together."

Whilice nodded slowly. "I wasn't really surprised. You always seem to be at the office when I'm not around."

I ignored his comment and looked at the roses. "They're pretty. Thank you. Can you put them in some water for me?" I was hoping he would leave right away to do that but I could tell by the look in his eyes that he had more to say. I closed my eyes, trying to send a clear message that I wasn't in the mood to hear anything. I just wanted to be alone.

Whilice never caught the hint, though. Either that or he caught it and chose to ignore it. He lay the flowers down and said, "So, did you get your work done?"

I sighed. "Most of it. I still have a few things to go over before the meeting."

"You do? But you were gone most of the afternoon and all evening."

"And your point?" I asked with a touch of indignation.

"No point. I'm just surprised that you didn't get everything done."

"Well, I didn't."

His lips curled and his eyebrows rose. "Hmmph."

"Hmmph what?" My hands were clenched tightly under the water. He was working my nerves in a way I just didn't need at that moment.

"Hmmph nothing. The girls missed you, that's all. They say they don't get to see you much anymore."

"I'll make it up to them."

"I missed you too."

I looked up at him, but didn't say a word. He stood up and went to the sink and looked at himself in the mirror. Why couldn't he have just left me the hell alone?

"Were you there alone?"

"Does it matter?"

"Just wanted to make sure you were safe."

"Well, I'm home, aren't I? And for the record, yes, I was there alone."

"Hmmph," he said again. Damn, he was working me.

"Hmmph what?" I asked louder than I intended.

"After we got home, the girls and I decided that it would be fun to pay their hardworking mother a visit. So we all hopped back in the car, made a pit stop at KFC, grabbed a bucket of honey barbecue, and stopped by."

I remained silent as I watched him watching me in the mirror. Was he bluffing?

"The guy who works for you, what's his name? Abraham somebody . . ."

"Lincoln."

"Yeah, yeah. Abraham Lincoln, like the president. Good ole Honest Abe."

"What about him?" I studied his eyes, searching for some type of indication as to what he did and didn't know. Since he didn't have an entrance badge, which was required to get into the building, I knew he couldn't have known much.

"He's married, right?"

"Yes. Why? And why the twenty questions?"

Whilice turned away from the sink, and came back to the tub and sat down. Then he put his hand in the water, and guided it in between my legs.

"Whilice, what are you doing?"

"I missed my wife," he said, trying to guide his fingers inside of me. "I miss making love to my wife, who works so hard."

"That's right, Whilice. I do. Someone in this house has to, right?"

He stopped with his fondling. "What do you mean by that?"

I groaned and pulled the stopper up so the water could drain. "Nothing, Whilice. I didn't mean a thing." I stood up and kept my parts covered as I grabbed my towel. I was uncomfortable as he stared at me.

"I work damn hard too, you know."

Damn! He just wouldn't give up. And I couldn't take it.

"Work hard? You mean settling is hard work?"

"What do you mean by settling?"

"Settling. S . . . E . . . T . . . T . . . L . . . I . . . N . . . G. That means that you are content to sit on your ass and do the bare minimum, while striving for nothing else."

"Nothing else? Do you know how hard my job is? Do you know how hard it is to sell cars now with the way the economy is?"

"Then find another job that's going to pay you some money."

"I make money."

"No, Whilice. You used to make money. Now you just bring home slightly more than what a manager in a damn fast-food restaurant does!"

"Why are you talking bullshit?"

I stepped out of the tub and threw on my silk robe. He had me fuming. I needed to take a shower this time, just to cool off. "I'm not talking bullshit, dear. I'm just talking truth. When I first met you, you were making almost double what you make now."

"Like I said, the economy's changed. People don't buy cars like that anymore."

"And like *I* said, get a different fucking job!"

"I don't need this shit, Taki. I bust my ass everyday, and I take care of *our* girls, which is more than you do.".

"Don't you even start that shit again!"

"Why? Because you don't want to hear the truth? Face it, Taki, you devote more time and energy to your job than you do your family. I mean damn, if you don't want to pay attention to me, that's fine, but at least give your girls some time."

"Whatever, Whilice. I give them time."

"No you don't, and you damn well know it!"

"That is bullshit!"

"Yeah, right."

"Damn it, I take care of them too, just like you do."

"Then why the hell are they missing their mother?"

I stepped past him and grabbed my brush from the sink. I felt like throwing it at him. Instead I said, "Will you please get the fuck out and let me have some privacy."

Whilice looked at me with some kind of evil in his eyes. I thought he was going to snap out and hit me. I gripped the brush just a little tighter just in case I needed to use it as a weapon. But rather than hit me, he just nodded his head and looked at me with the most black-hearted smile.

"Yeah, I'll get out," he said slowly. He turned and opened the door, but before stepping out, he stopped and with his back to me said, "Abraham Lincoln. I sold him a car once. This was before I met you. I remember him because of his name. I also remember him because of the license plate he said he was going to have made specifically for the convertible Benz that I sold him. *HnstAbe*. That's the same license plate that was on the back of the Escalade I saw parked next to your car earlier today."

He didn't say another word as he walked out and closed the door.

Abe

"What do you mean 'He knows'?"

I hadn't spoken or seen Taki for a little over a week since our last rendezvous because I had to go away to Dallas for a business conference. We were initially going to hook up there, but she changed her mind and said she needed time to think, which was cool with me, because after our last conversation, space was the one thing I wanted. Her talk of having deeper feelings for me freaked me out. Pissed me off, actually. We had talked too many times about keeping it strictly physical. Love and romance were never supposed to be part of the equation. But instead of following the game plan, she was getting wrapped up in the worst way.

Falling in love with me?

That was the one thing I didn't want to hear. My only hope was after having made it perfectly clear that I wasn't on the same page, she would get her head back on straight, and everything could go back to being business as usual.

When I got back from Dallas, I called her once to test the waters and see what her mind-set was going to be like. I had to know what I was or wasn't going to walk into when I went back to the office. She never answered her phone though, and she never called me back, which worried me a little. When it came to their emotions and not getting what they wanted, women could be vindictive as all hell. Shit, I've known brothers who've had their cars keyed up, clothes burned, cash spent, or worse, I've known women who have flipped out and become psycho like Lynn Whitfield did in *Thin Line Between Love and Hate.*

So when Taki stopped by my office and said she wanted to see me after hours, I was a little apprehensive about it. But I never walk away when the music's on, so I agreed to stay. I didn't quite know what to expect, but I was damn sure not expecting to hear what she told me when I walked in and closed her door.

"What do you mean 'He knows'?" I asked her again.

We were alone in her office. Lights on—bright; door closed, but not locked. This was not the kind of meeting I'd been hoping for.

"He saw your truck."

"How'd he know it was mine?"

"Your license plate."

"What about it?"

"Before he met me, he sold you a Mercedes-Benz. I guess in your conversation with him, you told him about getting personal plates."

I scratched my goatee and thought for a moment.

Then I remembered. "That's your husband? He looked different back then."

Taki curled her lips and said, "Yeah, he's changed a lot since then."

I let that go because I wasn't trying to step into her personal space. "So he saw my car. So what? I work here too. If he didn't see anything, then what's the problem?"

Taki got out of her chair and walked to the window. She was looking stressed. Her hair was wild and unkempt; she hardly had any makeup on, and looked like she hadn't been sleeping much. "I told him I was here alone."

"Okay, so why did he have an issue with that? So we were both here, that doesn't mean we saw each other."

"Abe, he knows we work together. Come on. He's not stupid."

I was frustrated. The last thing I wanted to do was deal with a jealous husband.

"Why didn't you just say that we were doing work? Why lie to him?"

"How was I supposed to know he was going to come here?"

"Doesn't matter. I told Nakyia I had to get information for you. I never said I would be alone. Cover all your bases, Taki . . . that's what you're supposed to do. The more you lie, the less you can cover."

She turned away from the window and glared at me. I could tell she wasn't happy with what I was saying, but shit, it was the truth. I always made it a point to be as truthful as I could with Nakyia. I may bend the truth a little here or there, or forget to mention certain things, but I never fabricated an entire lie. My philosophy was that the truth, oftentimes, made the best lies. Too bad Taki didn't realize that.

"I am not stupid," she said with a finger in the air and a twist of her neck.

"I never implied that you were. I just said to cover your back."

"You don't have to give me any lessons. I know how to cover my back."

I groaned and massaged my dome. She was giving me a headache. "Whatever," I said. "So what else did your husband say?"

"Nothing."

"Nothing?"

"Did I stutter? He said nothing. He just mentioned that he saw your car, and then left. We haven't spoken much since."

"We should cool things for a little while," I said. "Take a break before anything else can happen."

"Take a break? Why?"

"Come on, Taki. Your husband suspects something. I don't know about you, but I'm not trying to put my shit at risk for some ass."

"Some ass?"

Damn. My thoughts slipped out before I could close my mouth.

"Is that all I am to you? A piece of ass?"

"You know I didn't mean it that way. Don't act a fool."

"Oh, so now I'm a fool?"

"Taki, let's not go there, okay. What I said didn't come out the right way."

"Oh, I think everything sounded just fine. You said I was a piece of ass, and a fool."

"Damn Taki, let's chill with the attitude, all right."

She threw her hands up in the air. "Now I have an attitude?"

"I'm out of here," I said, turning around. My blood was starting to boil, and my head was getting warm. I had to leave before things got any worse; before I said more things I meant. Of course, that wasn't happening, because before I could open the door, she Demi Moore'd me.

"You're fired!"

My hand paused on the knob and I stood immobile. I just knew I didn't hear what she said. I turned and faced her. "What did you just say?"

"You heard me. I said you're fired."

It was my turn to snap.

"What the fuck do you mean *fired?* Why are you playing games?"

"Who's playing games? You are F . . . I . . . R . . . E . . . D . . . fired. You can move on to the next piece of ass."

"You can't do this shit."

"Can and just did. Maybe you forgot, but I am the boss. I can do and say whatever the fuck I feel like."

I watched her intensely, waiting for some indication that she was twisting my balls for a laugh. When she gave none, I said, "This is bullshit and you know it. You don't mean that."

"Oh, so now you're telling me what I do and don't mean?"

"Come on, Taki. Think about what we have going on. Why are you going to go and fuck with that?"

"You said you wanted a break; well, I'm giving you one. A nice long one."

"And your feelings for me?"

"Don't mean shit."

"That's a lie."

"No, Abe. That's not a lie. You told me to tell the truth, remember."

"After all of the shit I helped you do, how are you going to do that to me? Why? Just because I wanted to be careful?"

"No, it's not because of that. You love your wife, remember? Besides, I am nobody's piece of ass. I have more respect for myself than that. I thought you did too. Obviously I was wrong."

I slammed my hand against the door, causing plaques on her wall to slant. She jumped like she thought I was about to hit her. I slammed the door again. And then I made the dummy move. I said the one thing I shouldn't have.

"Why are you being a fucking bitch about things?"

She arched her eyebrows. "So now I'm a bitch? Security is still here. I think you better leave before I have them come and escort your ass out of here."

I was too mad to watch what I was saying or doing at this point. I couldn't believe I had gotten caught up like that. I flipped out and kicked her desk, causing her family photo to fall and shatter. I didn't give a shit. I kicked it again.

"That's it, I'm calling security."

Before she could start dialing, I snatched the receiver from her hand. I only wanted to talk, but she thought otherwise, and screamed and slapped me in my face. I reacted on instinct and pushed her away from me. Damn if she didn't fall right onto her broken frame.

"You son of a bitch!" she screamed. "Look at what you did to me. My hand is bleeding. Look at what you did!"

Shit.

I dropped the receiver and immediately knelt down beside her. I hadn't meant for that to happen. "Taki, are you okay? Shit, I didn't mean—"

"Didn't mean? You fucking pushed me down! Get the fuck away from me! Don't you dare put your hands on me again."

"Taki, I'm sorry. You hit me and I reacted. It was an accident. Let me help you."

"Abe, you better keep your hands off of me. I don't need or want your help."

I exhaled, stood up, and watched her as she held up her hand, which was barely bleeding. Damn, women could blow shit out of proportion.

I wanted to get the hell out of there so bad, but I couldn't leave without trying to change the course of the tidal wave that was hitting me. I counted backward from ten and then waited until she stood up before saying anything. When she did, I did the best thing I could think of doing: I kept my voice low and apologized.

"Taki, I'm sorry about your hand. I truly didn't mean for that to happen."

She looked at me with violent eyes and shook her head. There was obviously no avoiding the wipeout. She licked a small trail of blood from her palm and then reached for her purse. From the inside, she removed a stun gun.

"What's up with that?" I asked.

"Fuck you and your apology. I want you out of here now."

"I could fight this, you know," I said quietly. "I could say you sexually harassed me."

She held up her palm and smiled. "And I would turn that shit around and just tell them how you came on to me, and then knocked me down because I wouldn't have sex with you."

I nodded and bit down on my lip. It didn't surprise me that she had been willing to go there. I walked out of her office without a reply, refusing to lower myself any more than I already had.

After leaving the office, I drove down Collins Avenue with A Tribe Called Quest rapping from my stereo about how they knew how it felt to be stressed-out. I turned the volume up until it couldn't go anymore, and then I rapped right above their voices. I definitely knew how it felt. I'd fallen face-first into the pit that I had worked hard to avoid. The sad thing was that I had been digging it from day one, and knew it. Now I was out of a job, and to make matters worse, in the frame of mind that she was in, there was no telling what Taki would do. If she could pull a stun gun on me, which still tripped me out, and was willing to lie about what went down, then she could just as easily call my house and speak to Nakyia.

Women.

I grabbed my cell and called the house to test the waters. Thankfully they were still calm. I had woken her.

"When are you coming home, baby?" she asked with sleep heavy in her speech.

"Soon. I have to make a quick run to the store. You need anything?"

"Just you."

"How's the pain?"

"Never ending. But I'll live. I miss you."

"I miss you too."

"Baby, I want to talk to you when you get here. I have something I want to discuss with you."

My heart stuttered. Maybe a hurricane had blown through my home after the wave crashed, after all?

"What's up, lady?"

"We'll talk after you get here, sexy. We'll talk after we make love. Hurry home."

"I'll be there soon."

I hung up the phone and breathed a long sigh of relief. She wanted to make love. That meant that Taki hadn't completely bugged out and called her. I was safe for the time being. But I still had the issue of my employment status to deal with. How was I going to tell Nakyia that I'd lost my job? More importantly, what was my reason going to be?

The Tribe CD over, the changer switched to a CD I had in there for moments just like the one I was having. As Linkin Park raged, I vented right along with them about trying so hard, but only managing to get but so far. And how in the end, nothing I did really mattered.

I started the song over and screamed out again. With Taki firing me, I had definitely fallen; I just hoped that my talk with Nakyia wasn't going to be the start of my losing it all. I was about to start the song over again, when my cell vibrated in my lap. I checked the caller ID, and when I saw who it was, I lowered the music and answered.

"What's up, big brother?"

"Not much, Abe. What's up with you?"

"Not much. Just driving, releasing some stress."

"Oh yeah? You stressed-out too?"

"Sounds like you're having as good a time as I am," I said.

"Man, I'm having a great time," Randy answered sarcastically.

"What's up, man? I know you didn't call just to bullshit."

Randy sighed heavily into the phone. "No, I didn't call to BS. I called for a couple of reasons."

Stopping at a red light, I said, "'Sup, man."

"I need some advice. I fucked up big time."

"What happened?"

Another sigh. "Monique caught me with Tina last night."

"What! Get the fuck outta here! You fucked Tina? Why the hell would you go and do that?"

"Hold on, hold on. It really wasn't how it seemed. Tina and I didn't do anything. Well, not all that we could have."

I hit the gas as the light turned green. "Okay, back up. You have me confused."

As I took the long way home, I listened to all of the drama my big brother had been dealing with. It actually made me feel good to hear that I wasn't the only one going through some shit. I pulled into my driveway just as he was finishing his recap.

"Randy," I said, killing the engine. "I know you've heard this from me before, but why the hell don't you tell Tina to back the fuck off? Most women wouldn't put up with any of the shit that Tina pulls. Monique obviously loved your ass. Honestly, big brother, you're lucky she didn't break out sooner."

"I know, man. I just wanted to avoid having Jalisa go through the bullshit with parents who can't get along."

"Sometimes that's not always possible."

"I know."

"So what are you going to do about Monique and Tina?"

"I don't know what I'm gonna do about Monique. Shit, if I would have seen what she did, I wouldn't want to have anything to do with me, either. I've been trying to call her all day, but of course she's not answering. All I can do is hope that she'll eventually cool off enough to let me really explain what happened, and give me another chance."

"Yeah well, you'll never get that opportunity unless you get Tina in check."

"Yeah, yeah. I know. Abe, I swear that shit was the last straw with her. I'm tired of letting her intrude on my life. Jalisa can handle it."

"Now you're talking. Speaking of Jalisa, how is my beautiful niece handling Monique's departure?"

"She's sad about it, but she understands that Tina caused it. I swear, man, she's so grown it's scary. I can honestly say that I underestimated my little girl."

I smiled. "Little Jalisa. Man, you two need to make a trip here to Florida. Get away from the New York hustle and bustle."

"Yeah, that sounds like a plan. I think I could use the vacation right about now."

"How's the writing coming? When's the next book coming out? The last one was good, man. Serious, but good."

"It's going into print in the next couple of weeks. It's not as serious as the last one."

"Good stuff. So what was the other thing you wanted to talk to me about?"

"I spoke to Travis yesterday."

At the mention of his name, my mood instantly changed for the worst. I hadn't spoken to or thought of Travis in a long, long time.

"When's the last time you spoke to him, Abe?"

I clenched my jaws. "Randy, I love you, bro, so I'm gonna be nice when I say this . . . don't bring up that faggot's name to me again."

"He's your brother, Abe."

It was hard to control the rising volume and anger in my voice. "That faggot is not my brother!"

"Come on, man. I'm not big on his lifestyle either, but we all grew up together. We shared the same rooms, wore the same clothes, man. He's gay but he's our blood."

"Fuck that! I don't want to have anything to do with him. I told him that years ago. You were there and you know how serious I was."

"Abe, we were all a lot younger. We're grown men now. Don't you think it's time you accepted Travis? Why be like Pops? I think he could really use his brothers in his life. He's going through a lot of shit."

"Fuck what he could use. He chose that life, so let him deal with whatever shit comes his way.

Damn homo deserves whatever he gets. If you want to speak to him, you go ahead. Shit, go hang out with his faggot ass for all I care. I don't give a shit. I'll stay right on the sidelines with Pops while you support his parade."

"Man, it's not that I support his parade. You know I think it's just as unnatural as you do, but he's family. How can you continue to turn your back on him like that? Six years, Abe. Don't you think that's long enough?"

I slammed my hand down on my steering wheel. "Randy, forever wouldn't be enough time for me."

"Whatever, man. You need to change your stance."

"Not in this lifetime. Why'd you bring up his gay ass anyway?"

"I have to pick him up from the hospital tomorrow. He got into some crap with his boyfriend."

Just hearing the word *boyfriend* being used in the same sentence with Travis made me want to hit something. I always had my feelings about him when we were growing up, but when he actually came out of the closet, I couldn't take it. From that point on I knew that he would tell everyone and anyone about his sexual preference, and I couldn't handle that. I didn't want to deal with the stares and the questions.

Why is your brother gay?

Are you gay too?

I couldn't stand it. He was an embarrassment to both myself and my father, and unlike Randy, there was no way in hell we were going to be there to support or help him. God created man to be with and procreate with a woman, not with another man. It goes against everything that the Bible says. In my book, next to murder and pedophilia, it is the ultimate sin.

"Randy, whatever that pillow-biter got himself into, he deserved it and more."

"Don't say that, Abe."

"This conversation is finished, man. I gotta go inside to my wife and take care of my *manly* duties."

I hung up the phone without giving Randy a chance to say anything else. I was pissed. My mind went back to the moment I'd broken Travis's nose when he came back home after being gone for three days. I could have killed him that day, and if Randy hadn't pulled me off of him, maybe I would have.

Fucking faggot.

I counted to ten and then went inside, hoping that Nakyia wasn't still in the mood, because I sure as hell wasn't.

Travis

I was gay.

I'd been gay since I'd come out of my mother's womb, only I didn't know it until I was twelve. Growing up I'd always been different from all of the other boys in school. I never wanted to play their games or play with the same toys. I preferred Barbie over G.I. Joe. I liked red and pink as opposed to black and blue. I was never interested in being tough, and I never cared that I couldn't fight.

I was in the seventh grade when I realized I was gay. By seventh grade most of the boys I knew had at least kissed a girl once or twice. I was not one of those boys. I had never done it, and I never had thoughts about doing it. I was constantly asking myself why I wasn't "normal." Why didn't I like the things all guys seemed to like? Why didn't I walk the same, talk the same? Why was I so different from my brothers? Why did I look like a boy, but feel like a girl on the inside?

With the pressure of not feeling like a normal,

growing boy weighing down on my shoulders, I figured the only thing that was going to take that pressure away was to have some type of physical relation with the opposite sex. So I asked my best friend, Vanessa Richards, to fool around with me.

Everything changed after that.

As inexperienced as we were, Vanessa and I kissed, tongued, and fondled one another in search of my answer, and when we finished, I knew that I was nothing like all of the other boys.

I couldn't stand the feel of Vanessa's lips pressing against mine. The little bit of tongue action that she sloppily gave me, made my stomach turn, and fondling her breasts felt unnatural. While other boys in school talked about how much fun it was getting to first, second, and sometimes third base, I just found the whole act downright disgusting. I shared my feelings with Vanessa afterward, and just as I thought she wouldn't, she didn't take the dislike of the intimacy with her personally.

My best friend since kindergarten, Vanessa was the only person I felt like I could truly be myself around. I never worried about getting a scrutinizing stare when I played with her dolls. I was never ridiculed because I chose to pass on playing sports to jump rope. Vanessa accepted me for who I was and not who she thought I should have been.

After confiding in her, she suggested that I could have been gay. Of course, I disagreed with her. I was a boy, after all, and as my father and brothers always said and showed, boys were only supposed to be interested in girls. But when Vanessa broke down all of the things I was into and all of my "funny" ways, I started to really wonder if she could be right. I mean, yeah, I was very animated with my hands and neck when I spoke. And yeah, I thought LL Cool J's lips needed to be bronzed. But gay?

After minutes of going back and forth, I asked to fool around again. That was my first sexual encounter after all, and maybe I just needed to be schooled a little. After another awkward and unexciting kiss, however, it was obvious that I was a homosexual.

But even though I'd admitted the truth to myself, I still tried to do things in defiance of my feelings. I put down the dolls and tried to get used to playing with action figures. I tried being into girls and finding something attractive about them. I even tried flirting with them, but that never got me anywhere; they just ended up becoming my close friends. My time of self-denial lasted for about a year and after a year's worth of fighting, I gave in and finally came to grips with accepting reality.

Letting the person who'd been trapped inside of me out was one thing, but breaking the news about it to my family was another. So I decided to live in the closet for fear of them ever finding out. I knew how they—particularly my brothers and father—felt about gays, and I didn't want to have to deal with the stress and ridicule. To keep my secret safe, Vanessa and I pretended to date. Whenever we were around anyone, we made googly eyes and acted like typical teenagers in love. We held hands and gave each other kisses, which I always hated. When we were alone, we talked about all of the cute guys in school and wondered what it would feel like to have sex with a boy.

I lived that way until I was sixteen.

That's when I got tired of living a lie. Vanessa warned me not to say anything. She tried to tell me how things would get worse if I did; how my family would turn against me. She was such a good friend, that she actually suggested that we get married in the future and live together, that way I could have fun on the down low. But I just couldn't do that. I was so damn unhappy. So damn stressed-out. As each day passed, keeping my sexual preference hidden became a burden that was killing me slowly. I contemplated committing suicide so many times, but I just never had the guts to go through with it. I was falling deeper and deeper into a pit of depression, and I knew that the only way I was going to be able to survive was to come out.

"I'm gay."

We were having family dinner when I made my announcement. I sat dead still as my heart pounded in my chest, and waited for everyone's reaction, which turned out to be nothing but dead silence. "I'm gay," I said again as everyone stared at me.

Another tense couple of seconds crept by until finally something happened. Although she didn't speak, my mother, who'd been sitting next to me, took hold of my hand and gave me a smile. In that moment I could tell that she'd always known, and had just been waiting for me to come out. Holding my mother's hand in mine, I looked to my father, whose reaction was the complete opposite. With venom in his eyes, he cursed me, damned me, and rejected my existence as his seed. "You are not my son!" he raged. "I do not and will not have a faggot for a son!"

My mother tried to get him to calm down, but he was relentless and spat more insults at me, each one cutting me deeper than the one before. Unable to take the verbal bashing, I got up and left the house, and didn't go home for three days. It was during that time that I had my first sexual encounter.

After leaving the house, I'd caught the subway and headed to the Village in Manhattan and walked around aimlessly until my stomach rumbled, reminding me that I hadn't really eaten. I had just enough money for a burger and fries so I stopped at a small diner. I was sitting at the front counter alone eating when a white man in his midforties walked in and took the stool beside me. He wasn't the most attractive man. Truth be told, he was downright nasty. He was overweight, needed a shave, had bad skin, and smelled like old sausage.

I knew the moment I looked at him that he was gay and had a thing for me. He introduced himself as Bill, and spoke to me for a little while, telling me things about himself, before he started asking me questions about where I'd come from. I usually don't talk to strangers, but after the conversation I had at home, a conversation with a stranger just seemed like something I really needed.

The whole time Bill and I spoke, although he hadn't come out and said it directly, I knew what he wanted. Under normal circumstances, losing my virginity to a man like him would never have happened. But my father's hate-filled insults were bashing me over and over again in my head, and I was broken inside. I knew it was the wrong thing to do, but as unwanted as I was feeling at that particular moment, I finished my meal and left with the only person that wanted to love me. The fact that it wasn't real love meant nothing.

Bill took me to a hotel and paid for a room for three days. During those three days, I endured his funk, his weight, and his callousness, and experienced sex for the first time—all without a condom. Luckily, I didn't get an STD.

After the third day, Bill left and I went home and hoped that my father had somehow managed to calm down and would be willing to talk to me. I also wanted to talk to my brothers, whose reactions I hadn't yet received.

My father wasn't home, and from the look in my mother's sad eyes, it was obvious that his absence had been a good thing. Thankfully, she didn't ask me too many questions; she was just glad that I'd returned home. As I shed a river of tears, she hugged me tightly and told me that regardless of my sexual preference, I was and always would be her son. She didn't know it, but her words saved my life, because that whole ordeal had taken me to the edge and I was seriously considering giving it all up that night.

Just as she always did, my mother put together a hot plate of food for me to eat, which I did within seconds. After eating I went upstairs to face my brothers. I knew how they both felt about homosexuals, so I knew the likelihood of them damning me the way my father had was high, but I still held out hope for their understanding and support.

When I walked into the bedroom, my oldest brother, Randy looked at me and gave me a nod. He didn't speak, but he didn't need to. With his eyes, he'd told me that no matter what, I was his brother and he would have my back. My other brother, Abe, didn't speak to me either. Well, not until after he jumped up and broke my nose and bruised my ribs. Then, like my father, he called me a faggot and said I was no longer his blood.

I left the home I'd grown up in after that and went to live with Vanessa and her mother, who welcomed me with open arms. I stayed with them until Vanessa went off to college. And because I just barely managed to graduate, I never entertained the idea of following in her footsteps. I stayed with Vanessa's mother for a little while, but with her new boyfriend not happy with my presence and Vanessa not there to back me up, I eventually moved out.

With nowhere else to go, I went to live in the streets of Manhattan and prostituted myself. Some days the money was good, most days I made just enough to get a nice hot meal, and every day I dealt with danger of some kind, whether it be from gay bashers, police, or the clients themselves who loved to be physical. I can honestly say that those were some of the worst days I'd ever experienced.

Eventually, I got tired of living on the edge and being a stranger's piece of meat, and gave up the prostitution to do what I'd seen a lot of my gay compadres on the street do—get a sugar daddy. They were usually older men, married with families who wanted to but couldn't come out of the closet for fear of losing everything they had. For the first time, I actually had the upper hand in the "business arrangement." See, with me they were able to truly let loose and be themselves without being scrutinized, and since I was fulfilling their needs, they gladly fulfilled mine by supplying me with enough money to live comfortably without having to get a real job.

Having a sugar daddy was an almost perfect business deal. I scratched their backs, and they scratched mine until theirs no longer needed to be scratched. That was usually when the arrangement came to an end.

But there was one exception.

Married with four kids, Paul was a high-powered executive who worked in advertising. We met at a gay club one night in the city. Like all of the other arrangements before him, ours started out the same way: when he needed to be set free, he called me. Somewhere along the line however, things changed, and instead of calling on me only when he had an urge that needed to be satisfied, he would call me just to see how I was doing.

For the first time, I was experiencing a real relationship, as I'd finally met someone who wasn't just interested in only being satisfied. Paul genuinely cared about me and paid attention to me like no one ever had before, always taking the time to make me feel like the queen he always said I was. The more I saw him—which was never enough since he lived out of state—the harder I fell for him and his muscular physique, and handsome, yet rugged face.

Unfortunately, as perfect as he was, Paul had a tendency to get violent with me sometimes. I know he didn't mean to hurt me, though, because whenever he did, he always begged for my forgiveness and explained how stressed-out he was over the pressures at work, and more importantly, how being in love with me and having to live a lie was the hardest thing he'd ever had to do.

He'd put me in the hospital a couple of times, but this last time was the worst, as my arm and three of my ribs had been broken. My eye had also been blackened. I wish I could have called Vanessa instead of Randy, but I hadn't been able to do that since her fiancé, who was as homophobic as they come, demanded that she end her friendship with me or lose him. I couldn't be mad at her for having chosen her future husband over me; she'd done so much for me already.

I was fortunate to have the relationship that I did have with Randy. He may not have approved of my lifestyle, but just like he'd said with his nod years ago when I came out, he was always there. I don't know why, but despite the hatred in his words and actions, I still held out hope that one day Abe would have been there too. As for my father—well, I wasn't even going to kid myself. I knew he could have cared less if I had died.

"You didn't tell Ma, did you?" I asked, painfully getting into Randy's car.

"She doesn't know."

"Good. The last thing I need is for her to be worrying about me." I grunted as I closed his door.

My ribs were sore and breathing was difficult. Randy looked at me and gave me a disapproving frown. I rolled my eyes.

"Randy, please don't give me any speeches. I've had a rough night. I just want to get home and get some rest."

"Travis, man, why do you put up with Paul's shit? I mean, how much longer are you going to allow him to use you for a punching bag? Shit, man, look at you. Your eye is fucked up. Your ribs are busted, your arm broken. Is he really worth it?"

I looked away from Randy and stared out the window. The sky was overcast with gray clouds as rain was coming. The clouds in the sky reflected my mood. I was hurting more than I wanted my brother to know.

"Travis, look, I know you think this guy loves you—"

"He does," I said, trying to fight back tears that were forming in my eyes. "He does Randy, okay. He's just stressed. He's living in the closet and that's not an easy thing to do. I know. I've been there. I know what it's like to live a lie and never be truly happy because you can't just be yourself. Putting on fake smiles for the world to see, pretending to be something and someone you're not."

"Then tell him to come out of the closet, man. If he's so stressed that he's beating your ass every five minutes, tell him to come out."

"He can't!"

"Why?"

"He just can't!" I wiped my falling tears away with my good arm. Randy and my mother knew about Paul, but they didn't know that he was married. I kept that information from them, because I knew they would have had serious issues with that.

"Why can't he?"

I turned and faced my brother, not caring that he saw my tears. "Randy, coming out of the closet is one of the hardest things for a gay person to do. When gays make a decision like that, it's done knowing that their whole life will change. There's the ridicule, the sudden lack of respect that people have. The anger and fear that people develop overnight. Friends who claim to be your friends abandon you. Family that you used to be close to and whose support you used to have, will put you down, hurt you physically and mentally, and throw you out like moldy leftovers.

"That's how the world is, big brother. And that's what Paul wants to avoid. He has a good, high-paying job. If he came out, he would probably lose that and his reputation would be damaged. Whether you like it or not, I love him and I don't want him to go through any of that. I lost most of my friends and family the instant the words 'I'm gay' came flying out of my mouth. I know how bad it hurts."

I watched my brother through my tear-filled eyes. My head hurt from my own painful memories of my loss.

"Randy, I lost my father, my brother, and eventually my best friend. You and Ma are the only family I have left. How can I want Paul to go through the same thing?"

"Travis, I know your life hasn't been easy. I know that losing Pops and Abe hurts. But as bad as it hurts, you've survived. If Paul loves you like you say he does, he'll survive too. Look at yourself, Travis. This isn't the first time you've looked like this, and I know it's not going to be the last. Love and be loved. That's what we all want in this world. Man, you're doing all the loving and getting nothing in return but hospital fees. Don't you think it's time that changed? Don't you think it's time Paul came out or you moved on?"

I didn't respond for a few seconds as I sat quiet and digested the things he'd said to me. I'd actually given Paul an ultimatum once about coming out of the closet. But the only thing that did was trigger a physical assault from him, and then I didn't hear from him for several months, and his absence had just been too much for me to bear. In answer to Randy's question, yes, I wanted the situation to change, but I didn't want to lose the one person who made me feel loved. I was somebody important to Paul, not just a piece of ass.

"Can I ask you something?" I said, looking back through the glass now being pelted with raindrops. I watched my distorted reflection as my tears fell and cascaded down with the raindrops. "Why didn't you desert me? Why do you continue to be there for me? Ma does it because I'm her child. She bore me and she would never leave me, or any of us. But you . . . You could have been like Dad and Abe. I know how you feel about my lifestyle. I know you disagree with it and hate it. So why have you always been there for me?"

I listened to the melody the rain played on the top of Randy's Camry. It was a sad song filled with pain and abandonment—my song.

Randy sighed. "You're right, Travis, I don't and have never really liked that you're gay. But whether I like it or not, that's who you are. You're Mom's seed, but you're also my baby brother. You were the little kid I watched out for when we were younger because you couldn't kick your way out of a paper bag. The little kid who couldn't sleep at night without the night-light. The little kid who was always different. For better or worse, you will always be my baby brother. I can't desert you. Now as for the lifestyle you've chosen . . . I hate that more than I do the fact that you're gay."

"I had no choice, Randy. I had no home."

"You could have tried to do something else, Travis. You didn't have to choose to live on the streets. You didn't have to give yourself up for spare change. And you don't have to stay with someone who can't keep his fists off of you."

I frowned. "I'd take Paul's fists over family's any day."

"It wasn't an easy thing to accept, Travis. Abe reacted the only way he knew how to at the time."

"You didn't hit me."

"Abe and I are different."

"How is my older brother doing, anyway?"

"He's doing well. I gave you the number. Have you tried to call him?"

"Randy," I said, watching the lighting flash sporadically throughout the sky. "I tried a long time ago. He didn't want to hear anything I had to say then and I know he doesn't want to now."

"What about Pops?"

I sucked my teeth. "Do you know that Ma has to

sneak off to another room and whisper when she talks to me?"

I turned and faced him. I wanted him to see the pain in my eyes; the hurt in my tears.

"To this day, she can't speak to her own son without Dad yelling at her. He still calls me a faggot. Did you know that? He won't refer to me as anything but that. He wouldn't give me the time of the day if I paid him. Six years ago, Randy. I was sixteen when I came out. I've lived a thousand lifetimes since then. I'm gay, big brother, but I'm still the same Travis they knew before I made my announcement."

Almost as if on cue, lightning flashed and thunder boomed so heavily I could feel the vibration in the car. Randy didn't say a word, and I had nothing more to say. We sat in silence for several seconds, listening to the storm's cacophony. As a new wave of tears fell, I said, "Start the car and take me home."

Randy

Jalisa was sound asleep when I got home after dropping Travis off. I didn't mind because it gave me a chance to have some time to myself to think. After paying my neighbor's granddaughter her babysitting fee, I turned off the lights, put a Najee CD on and slumped down in my living room sofa. Since the debacle with Tina, I'd tried to get Monique to talk to me, but had no luck. She'd literally caught me with my pants down and no matter how much I begged and pleaded she didn't want to hear a word I had to say. But I still tried regardless, because the fact was, I didn't really do anything with Tina. I mean yes, I'd come damn close, but I did put a stop to what was happening before things had gotten out of hand. As mad as Monique was, I just couldn't give up trying to make her understand how much I needed her and how my world just wasn't the same without her. Without her I was lost and empty. Without her my motivation to write was gone.

The only thing that kept me going was my

daughter. No matter how cloudy my days were, Jalisa always managed to bring a smile to my face. Sometimes it was hard to believe that such an angel could have been created with such a bitch like Tina. With all her good looks, she's by far one of the ugliest women I've ever known. After her stunt the other night, I'd had it; I wasn't going to let another day or night go by without putting a stop to all of her shit. That's why I had called her before I went to get Travis from the hospital.

"Randy, baby, I knew you'd call me. You want me to come over and finish what I started."

"Save it, Tina. I'm not in the mood for your shit."

"Don't snap at me, Randy. I didn't ask that bitch to come and spoil our party."

"There was no fucking party, Tina."

"I didn't see you complaining when I had your dick in my mouth."

I clenched and unclenched my hand. "Look, I've tried to keep things cool between us for Jalisa's sake, but I can't fucking take it anymore. I'm done with your fucking meddling, I'm done with your fucking attitudes, and I'm done with the fucking disrespect you show me and Monique!"

"So what are you trying to tell me, Randy?" Tina asked with a lot of attitude and indignation. "I hear a whole lot of rambling, but what are you saying?"

"What I'm saying, Tina, is that the days of you and your bullshit are over. No more two o'clock in the morning visits, and no more midnight calls. As a matter of fact, don't call here unless it legitimately has to do with Jalisa. And I don't mean your bullshit calls about how she's doing, because we all know you don't really give a shit about her. Now as far as you just stopping by to see her . . . that shit is over with. If you want to see your daughter, you'll have to wait until it's your turn to have her. Any other time, I swear you better fucking call ahead of time, because if you don't, trust me when I tell you that it'll just be a wasted trip for you."

"I'm sure it all sounds good to you, Randy, but do you really think you can stop me?" Tina asked arrogantly.

"It's not about thinking I can, Tina. I just will. Now as far as Monique goes—"

"What about that yellow bitch? She's out of the picture now."

I bit down on my lip and balled my hand into a tight fist. "You may have won the last round against Monique, but I'm telling you now that's the last round you'll ever win."

"Whatever," Tina cut in. "She's gone. So as far as I'm concerned, you're releasing nothing but hot air."

"Tina, as much as you may not want to hear this, I am going to get Monique back because *she* is the one for me. Are you listening to me? *Monique* is my soul mate. Not you. Not ever. She and I were meant to be together and when that happens, I'm telling you now, you better respect it."

Tina sucked her teeth. "Whatever."

"Yeah, whatever. You just make sure to keep your shit in check." I hung up the phone seething, but feeling relieved at having finally let off some steam. It had been a long time coming. I'd held my feelings back for far too long, and now that I had released myself of some tension, I was even more determined to get Monique back into my life. Somehow, I had to get her to hear me out.

I dozed off to Najee's melody and woke up when my phone rang. I looked at the time; it was nearing eleven. I wanted it to be Monique, but unfortunately it wasn't. "What's with the late call, Travis? You in trouble again?"

Travis sighed dramatically. "No, I'm not."

"So what's up?"

"I called to say thank you. The talk we had meant a lot to me."

"No problem, man. I know things aren't easy for you and we don't necessarily see eye to eye, but I just want you to be happy. Ultimately that's what it's all about."

"I wish Abe and Dad could look at it that way."

"Maybe someday they will."

"When I'm dead, maybe."

"Come on, man. Chill with that talk, all right."

"Whatever. Anyway, I just wanted to say thanks and to tell you that you were right: I do deserve more than what Paul is giving me. It wasn't easy for me to come out of the closet but I did because I didn't want to live a lie. I want my partner to be the same way. I'm going to tell him that."

"That's good to hear, Travis. Hopefully things work out the way you want them to."

"Somehow Randy, I don't think they will. But whatever. I just don't want to be someone's secret anymore. I'll talk to you later."

"All right, Travis. Hey, be careful out there, all right. And I'm here if you need me."

"Thanks, big brother. Hey, how're Jalisa and Monique?"

"They're good. Jalisa's sleeping right now. You need to come and see her sometime."

"Yeah, maybe I'll do that. I'll see you around."

I hung up the phone and sighed. Accepting my brother's choice wasn't the easiest thing for me to do. Sometimes when I sat and dwelled on it, his being a homosexual really bothered me. To know that he got intimate with another man made my skin crawl. I don't think there's anything natural about it. Since the beginning of time, the rule has always been man + woman = child. I don't know where, when, or why that equation was altered, but like it or not, the reality is that it had been.

Even though I have a problem with it, I couldn't turn my back on Travis. When he first came out of the closet I used to wonder sometimes if I'd done something wrong as a big brother.

Had I not steered him in the right way?

Did I not set the right examples?

I know my father dealt with the same internal questions, because I could see it on his face. I think he feels as though he failed Travis in some way. He actually once said that Travis's being gay was punishment for something he had or hadn't done. But as I'd gotten to talk with him and hear his side of things over the years, I knew Travis's being gay had nothing to do with any mistakes any of us made. That was just who he was. Again, I don't know why the equation had changed, but I guess when you really broke it down, there were worse things in the world than being gay.

I wish Abe and my father could have found a

way to get past their judgment of Travis and his lifestyle and just be there for him like I did. Like it or not, he was our blood. He was part of all of us. I have to give credit to my mother though, because she could have disowned Travis too. With all of the drama she's had to deal with from my father, it would have been easier for her to have done just that. Ever since Travis came out and my mother accepted him, my father stopped treating her with the same respect that he once had. It was tough to sit by and watch it happen sometimes. On more than one occasion I'd almost lost my cool and gone off on him for yelling at her and putting her down, but every time I came close, my mother would calm me down.

"This is my battle to deal with, Randall. Not yours."

"But Mom, his disrespect for you is ridiculous."

"He's angry inside, that's all."

"And that's an excuse to let him treat you the way he does?"

"Trust me, he doesn't mean anything by it. I'm just the only person he has to let his frustration out on. Just stay quiet about it and let me handle him like I've been doing."

I disagreed with my mother's methods of dealing with my father's bitterness, but I always did as she asked, and stayed quiet.

I got up from the couch, turned the stereo off, and I went to Jalisa's bedroom to check on her. Although she flashed the same smile every day, I knew that since Monique had gone, she hadn't been the same. In a lot of ways, they'd become like mother and daughter. She loved Tina regardless of how much of a bitch she was, but I knew that Monique was who she looked up to. I stared at her for a few more seconds and then closed the door and went to bed, determined to bring Monique back into both of our lives.

Abe

I sat in my VP's office waiting for him to finish with his business call. I'd been out of work for two days. I'd told Nakyia I was taking a much needed mini-vacation. After my blowup with Taki, I went home and sat in my living room and thought about what my options were. I thought about filing a suit against her, but to do that meant that Nakyia would know I was cheating on her and I wasn't willing to have that happen, because I wasn't willing to lose my wife. I tried calling Taki, to see if she had finally calmed down and come to her senses, but she never answered her phone and didn't return any of the messages I'd left for her at work or on her cell. To save my job, I was left with only one option. And that's why I was in Brian's office.

I looked around at the numerous degrees he had hanging on his walls. He was an educated man, with both his bachelor and master's degree in business. He'd been in advertising for twenty years, and at forty-five, was the only minority to hold a VP position with the company. I had a good working relationship with Brian. I'd golfed with him and a few other people from work, and I had been to his house for picnics and met his family.

I looked at the family photograph he had on his desk. His two boys are his spitting image. His wife is a beautiful natural sister with mocha skin and Nubian locks and could have been a model, but instead of using her beauty, she used her brain and was an attorney like Nakyia.

I went to Brian because I didn't think he'd hesitate to help me out with my situation since I was the only one that knew he was cheating on his wife. I discovered his secret when I accompanied him on a business trip to New York one time. Taki was supposed to go, but she had gotten sick so I took her place.

We stayed at the Waldorf-Astoria in Manhattan. After having a business dinner in the lounge with some potential clients, we went up to our rooms. Around one o'clock in the morning, my phone rang. It was Brian.

"Abe, sorry to bother you, but I need a favor."

Half-asleep I said, "What's up?" Knowing what a workaholic he was, I figured he wanted me to get some report or something for him, but work was hardly the thing he was working on.

"I was so busy before we left that I forgot to bring condoms with me, and my *friend* doesn't have any. Do you have any I could borrow?"

Caught off guard by his request, I stayed quiet for a few seconds. "Condoms?" I finally said.

Brian chuckled. "Look Abe, we're both grown men. Yes, I have a wife, but I also have needs that she can't fulfill. You're a married man, so I know you understand how stressful being married can be."

"Yeah . . . I do."

"Good. So I can trust that you will keep this between you and me, right?"

"Yeah," I said.

"Good. Now do you have any condoms?"

Because I hadn't yet begun to fool around on Nakyia, I didn't have any condoms to give him. We never spoke about that night after that and I never really thought I would need for him to return the favor. I was banking on it now, though.

Brian finally hung up the phone and rocked back in his leather chair. He resembled Sidney Poitier with fewer wrinkles and less gray hair.

"What's up, Abe? You ready for another round of golf? The fellas and I are going to Atlanta for a golf tournament this weekend."

"Count me in," I said.

"Good. I was hoping you'd say that. So anyway, what brings you by? And where have you been these past couple of days?"

I cleared my throat and got right down to it. "Brian, I have a situation and I need your help."

"Sure thing. There's always a solution."

"It's a little complicated, Brian, and to be honest it's going to require for you to have my back the way I had yours in New York."

Brian looked at me and nodded slowly. "What's going on?"

"I've been seeing someone on the side, and things got kind of ugly a few days ago, and now I've been fired."

"Fired? What are you talking about?"

"I've been sleeping with Taki, Brian."

He put up his hand for me to pause and then picked up his phone. After telling his secretary to hold all of his calls, I gave him the rundown on my entire relationship with Taki, and then told him about everything that happened in her office.

Taki

I waited until everyone, including Brian, left for the evening and then headed to my car. Abe was parked next to me and was leaning against his Escalade, waiting for me. I walked straight up him.

"You piece of shit!" I spat, my face inches away from his. "I can't believe you went to Brian and told him about us. Who the hell are you to put my business out like that?"

Abe stared at me evenly. "You left me no choice, Taki. I didn't deserve to be fired and you know that. Did you really think I would let you take my job away from me?"

"You threw me to the damn ground!"

"Come on, Taki. You know that's not how things went down. You were the one who flipped out by hitting me. I reacted out of instinct, but I didn't mean for you to fall."

"Brian roasted me and put me on temporary probation."

Abe shrugged his shoulders at me. "I did what I had to do to keep my job."

"I could tell your wife, you know," I threatened.

"Not unless you want me to confirm your husband's suspicions."

I threw my hands in the air and walked around to my car. "I should have never messed with your ass!" I fumbled with my key trying to get it into the lock. The darkness outside wasn't helping me any, neither was my anger and embarrassment over what happened in Brian's office.

"Taki," Abe said, coming beside me. "All I said was maybe we should chill for a little bit to avoid any drama from your husband that we both don't want or need."

He took my hand in his and turned me around. The scent from his Ralph Lauren cologne was making me moist. A good scent on a man has always been an aphrodisiac for me. Abe leaned into me and instinctively, my arms wrapped around his waist.

I took a quick look around to make sure that we were alone.

"You don't want any drama, do you?" Abe asked me soothingly.

I wanted to push him away because I was still pissed, but I felt powerless against his magnetism.

"I just want you, Abe," I said, giving into my desire.

He kissed me deeply, caressing my tongue with his. I knew it was about sex for him. He wasn't falling like I was. I took his hand and guided it under my blouse for him to caress my breasts, and moaned as he massaged me in a way only he could. Reaching my hand in between his legs, I felt his manhood come to life. Suddenly, he pulled away.

"Is our understanding intact?" he asked, looking at me with a dead-even glare.

"You mean, can I fuck you without any emotional attachment?"

"I just want to know if our understanding is intact."

Knowing that I wasn't going to be able to flick the switch on the feelings I had for him, I lied and said yes, and then grabbed him and pulled him toward me. We deep-throated for a second or two before going back to my office. I would deal with how much I was falling in love with him later.

"Taki, I want to talk to you."

I'd just hurried past the living room where Whilice had been watching TV, trying to get upstairs to jump into the shower. I needed to wash off the sweat and funk Abe and I created during the bout of angry sex we'd had.

I paused with my hand on the banister, and with my back to him said, "Whilice, I've had a long, rough day. I'm tired and all I want to do right now is go upstairs and take a shower."

I started up the stairs again, hoping he would leave me alone, but instead, he followed behind me.

"Taki, we need to talk. Now," he said, stepping into the bedroom behind me.

I turned and looked at him. His no-nonsense tone was surprising, and ticked me off a bit. I wanted to say something, but with the funk emanating from me, I held my tongue. "Let's talk after I bathe," I said.

"Why don't I join you?" Whilice asked.

"I'd really rather be alone."

"Look Taki, I know you're upset about the other night. That's what I want to talk to you about."

I watched my husband. Was he about to start talking about Abe again?

"Whilice, there's really nothing to talk about." I slipped out of my shoes and rested my keys on the dressing table.

"Yes there is, Taki. Look, I just want to say that I'm sorry for the way I came at you that night. I know that you take your job seriously and I shouldn't have been insinuating anything about you and Abe. The truth is that's his job too and he has every right to be there as you do. I'm sorry for making you feel as though I don't trust you."

I removed my jewelry and breathed a slow sigh of relief. "Thank you, Whilice," I said softly. "I appreciate the apology."

Figuring that was the end of things, I started to make a move to the bathroom. Before I could get there, Whilice moved toward me and grabbed me by my wrist and pulled me toward him.

"Whilice, I really need to take a shower."

"Come on, baby. It's been a while since we made love. Let me give you a real reason to jump in that shower."

I tried to push him away as he leaned in closer to me.

"Whilice, the girls will hear us."

He shook his head. "No, they won't. I sent them to my mother's house for the night. We're all alone."

Damn.

"After I bathe, Whilice," I said, unsuccessfully fighting him off.

"I want you now, baby."

He threw his arms around my waist and kissed me on my neck. Then he paused, and I heard him sniff. "Baby, what cologne is that?"

Damn.

"I stopped at the mall after work. I was trying to find you cologne. What you're smelling is a combination of the samplers I tried."

He sniffed again. "Ralph Lauren. Aren't you supposed to spray the sample on your wrist?"

"I had sprayed so much on my wrists that I started using my neck."

He sniffed again. "Smells nice."

I said a silent *thank-you* as I narrowly escaped with my quick thinking. I finally managed to push him off of me.

"Let's do this after I shower, okay," I tried again.

Whilice wasn't trying to hear that, though. "I don't want to wait. I want my wife now."

Before I could utter another protest, he grabbed me and pulled me with him on the bed. I squirmed, trying to get him to stop, but he was persistent. He pressed his hard crotch into my leg.

"Feel that, baby. It wants you. He's dying for you, and so am I." Whilice passed his hand along my calf and then up and over my thigh. Frantically, I tried to push him away, because I'd had to take my panties off after Abe had gotten through with me.

"Come on, Whilice, please, baby. I'll ride you good after I shower. I promise," I said as tears leaked from the corners of my eyes.

There I knew there was no way of getting out of the predicament I was in.

"Please, Whilice," I tried again, weakly.

But he wasn't listening. I took a deep breath, and relaxed myself, and waited for the storm to come as my husband slid his hand under my skirt.

"What the fuck?" Whilice stared down at me. "Where's your underwear?"

I didn't answer him right away.

"Taki," he said, his voice deepening, becoming venomous. "I asked you a question. Where the fuck is your underwear?"

"I . . . in my purse."

"Your purse? What the fuck are they doing in there?"

Tears fell as I remained silent. Whilice looked at me and then shook his head.

"Please tell me this isn't what I think it is." He pleaded at me with his eyes. I had to look away.

He suddenly put his hand back in between my legs, feeling inside of me with his fingers. I watched the pupils of his eyes darken as he removed his hand and shook his head again. Then he brought his fingers to his nose.

I don't remember much of anything but the slap across my cheek and the words, "bitch!"

Whilice jumped off of me. "You fucking whore! You have been fucking him!"

I didn't say anything as my cheek stung and my tears fell. Whilice had never laid his hands on me before. Never even come close.

"Bitch! You goddamned bitch! What the fuck did I do to deserve this? All I ever did was treat you right and take care of you and the girls." His eyes began to water. "I fucking love you!" he yelled. He came back to the bed and grabbed me by my shoulders. "Tell me, Taki, how could you do this to me? How could you fuck him?"

"Think about it," I said weakly.

"Think about what?"

"This is all your fault."

"My fault?"

"Yes, your goddamned fault!" I screamed. "You pushed me to him! You with your lazy, under-achieving ways. You don't bring any money into this household. You don't even try. You think I married you so that you could work half-ass during the day and then come home and sit on your ass, letting yourself go to waste. Look at me, Whilice, and look at you. Look at how you let yourself go. This is your fault. You and you alone."

He pushed me down and spat on me. "Bitch!" he said, standing up. "I've had it with you. I'm tired of you always putting me down. So I don't make as much as you, so fucking what! I don't see you spending time with the kids. I don't see you taking care of them. Money isn't everything, you know. I'm happy doing what I'm doing. I'm not underachieving. If I want to make more money I'll do that. But raising the girls and spending time with them is more important to me than busting my ass all day, every day, which is what I thought you were doing. I see now what you were busting your ass on. So how long have you been fucking him?"

I rose up from the mattress. "Long enough to know I'd rather have him inside of me than you."

Whilice slapped me again, causing me to fall

from the bed to the floor. I sat on the floor crying and holding my cheek. After a few seconds, I looked up at my husband. "Do you feel better?" I asked. "Do you feel like a fucking man now?"

Whilice looked down at me and suddenly his dark eyes became placid as his shoulders slumped. "When did you become such a bitch, Taki. You're not the woman I married."

"Yeah, well you're not the man I married, so we're in the same boat."

"Not anymore," he said with finality in his voice. "As of now, I'm officially jumping ship."

Whilice turned and without another word to me, walked out of the room. When I heard his car start and then back out of the driveway, I went into the bathroom to take the shower I desperately needed. I stood stoic as the water cascaded over my body, and cried for allowing myself to fall in love.

That night, alone in my bed, I thought about how my life was going to change. I'd lost my husband and I was possibly going to lose my girls. If anything, I would lose their trust and admiration. I cried myself to sleep that night and felt like a fool as I realized what I had irresponsibly been willing to lose.

Pipe dreams.

That's all my hopes with Abe had ever been.

Pipe dreams with no chance of ever becoming reality.

Travis

When Paul walked through my door I wanted to wrap my arms around him, but I held back. We'd spoken on the phone a lot since the last time he'd put me in the hospital. As usual, he apologized for what he'd done, and expressed yet again how his lashing out had to do with his growing frustrations about wanting to come out of the closet, but not being able to.

"It would ruin my career, Travis. All of the hard work and time I put into it, would be gone the minute I revealed my sexual preference. The relationships with my contacts would suffer. I'd lose the respect of my peers. I just don't want to go through that. These people know me as a hard-working, diligent, and reliable man. If I come out, they'll stop seeing me in that light, and they won't trust me.

"But besides the people I work with, there's also the matter of my family . . . especially my boys. You don't know what it's like to have sons looking up to you. I'm their idol, their role model. If I came out it would devastate them and I just can't do that to them. I love them too much to cause them pain that way."

I felt for Paul.

I really did.

But like I'd told Randy, I was ready to make my ultimatum because quite frankly, I'd had enough of the sad song. If he wanted to be unhappy, then he could be unhappy without me. But if he wanted to live a life without shackles, then he would have to choose to make his great reappearance to the world. With either decision there'd be crosses to bear and someone would get hurt, because as far as I'd experienced, happiness never came free of charge. Like I said, I felt for him and his dilemma. But I was tired of being his whipping boy. It was time to truly become his man or just become his memory.

After a few gentle kisses hello, we sat at my table where I had his favorite dish waiting—stewed chicken with rice and beans and salad on the side. He brought white Zinfandel. We ate over candlelight and music in near silence and when we were finished, we held hands and made small talk. I drank in his manly features, fearing for the first time a life without him. Was I truly prepared to deal with him choosing the closet and his coworkers and family over me? I'd invested so much into him.

My time.

My energy.

My love.

My blood.

Damn it, I know his decision wasn't an easy one to make, but wasn't I worth it?

I pulled my hand away from his.

"Paul, I need to say something."

He smiled at me. "What's up, queen?"

I blushed. I loved when he called me that.

I took a deep breath and let it out. "I'm not going to beat around the bush. I need you to make a decision. Either me or the closet."

Paul's smiled immediately disappeared. "What do you mean?"

"I mean I can't go on being your secret anymore. I'm tired of it. I want all of you, not a third. I don't want to be your part-time lover anymore. I want you to come out of the closet. If you can't, then I'm moving on."

"Travis, we've discussed this already. I have a wife and sons who look up to me. I have my reputation as a man. Damn it, my job and life are stressful enough as it is. I'm tired of going over this with you again and again. You're supposed to help me escape my problems, not cause more."

"I'm not trying to cause you more problems, Paul. I just want to be fair to myself and fair to you."

"Fair to me? How the hell is you giving me an ultimatum being fair?"

"Don't think of it as an ultimatum. Think of it as me giving you a chance to be truly happy."

Paul laughed. "That's really funny, Travis."

"There's so much more that I could give you, Paul, if you'd just open that door and let the world know who you are."

He stood from the table. "I know who the hell I am."

I slammed my palm down on the tabletop. "Then be with me!"

"I'm tired of this shit, Travis. I don't need this."

I shook my head. I had wanted to talk rationally about things, but at the rate we were going, things were going to get physical again. I didn't want to go to the hospital but I couldn't and wouldn't back down.

"Then what do you want to do, Paul? You want to leave? You want to give me up?"

"You're leaving me no choice."

"Fine. Since it's that easy for you."

"It's not easy. But neither is coming out."

"Well, don't worry about that anymore. You've obviously made your damn decision."

"Don't raise your voice at me, Travis."

"Oh, don't worry Paul, I won't. Believe me, I don't want to go to the hospital again."

"I wasn't threatening you."

"You don't have to!"

I stood up with tears threatening to brim in my eyes. I clenched down on my jaws and fought them back down, determined to not break down and cry in front of him. I took a breath to compose myself as my hands were shaking out of fear and anger. "Paul, before we go down our familiar road again, why don't you just get your things and leave. As a matter of fact, let me get your coat for you."

I walked away from the table and walked slowly to the closet. It was over. I'd given him a choice, he made it, and now it was over. I grabbed his coat and was taking it off of the hanger, when I noticed his wallet fall from his pocket to the floor. I picked it up and looked over my shoulder at Paul, who was swallowing down the rest of his wine. He hadn't seen anything. I looked at the wallet and then back at him, and then slid it into my pocket.

"Here," I said, tossing his coat to him.

"Travis, why don't we talk about this?"

"There's nothing to talk about. You made your decision and now I'm making mine. Get out." I walked to the door and opened it.

"Just like that?"

"Just like you made it," I said.

"I pay for this apartment you have, you know?"

I sucked my teeth and pursed my lips. "Don't worry, I'll leave."

"I'm not asking you to leave."

"Well then, I'll get a job and pay the rent my damn self."

"Can you just give me some time?"

"You've had enough, and now it's expired. Good-bye."

"Your loss," Paul said, walking past me.

I slammed the door shut and then dug in my pants pocket and removed the wallet. "We'll see who loses what," I said opening it and eyeing a wad of twenty-dollar bills.

I pocketed all fifteen that were in there and was about to pocket the few gold and platinum credit cards he had also, when I paused and thought about what I was doing. When the wallet initially fell, I'd made up my mind that I was going to take whatever was in it and take myself on a very nice shopping spree. But as I looked at the cash and cards, I thought about how easily Paul had walked away from me, and realized for the first time that he never truly loved me. If he had, he would have never been able to let go of what we had—or at least what I thought we had.

With the light having finally broken through the black clouds, I decided right then and there that I didn't want anything else from him. I took the cards and went to my window and threw them out, and watched them fall twelve floors to the street below to be found. I'm sure someone could put them to good use.

I won't lie . . . I did keep the cash. I was done with him, but that was three hundred dollars!

I tore up the rest of the miscellaneous papers in the wallet and removed his license to rip up and throw away also. But before I did, I took a quick glance at it; I just wanted to see his face one last time. However, my quick glance turned into a very long, unbelieving, bewildered stare. I opened and closed my eyes, thinking that maybe I'd seen something wrong. But I hadn't.

Monique

My cell phone rang again, making it the third time in the past three hours it had done that. I looked at ID screen; just like the last time, Randy's number was there. He just wouldn't give up. I grabbed my phone and thought about answering it. I missed him badly. Maybe just one time I would speak to him.

Maybe.

But before I could answer it, the call ended. I put the phone down and went back to doing the reminiscing I was doing before the call. That's all I seemed to be doing lately.

Thinking about old times with Randy and Jalisa.

Thinking about the happiness they brought to me.

Thinking about the way they made me smile.

Thinking about the completion I felt when I was with them.

Thinking about the future that I envisioned.

I couldn't stop thinking about any of those things and more, and honestly, I didn't want to stop. I sighed and promised myself that the next time he called I would answer, because it was time to stop thinking. An hour later the phone rang again and I didn't hesitate.

"What do you want, Randy?" I said with attitude; I was ready to give us another chance, but I wasn't about to make it easy for him.

"Hi, Monique!"

"Jalisa?"

"Yup," she answered back sweetly.

A smile immediately formed from my lips. "How are you, little lady?"

"Fine. I miss you."

"I miss you too," I said.

"How come you don't live here anymore? Did I do something wrong?"

I sighed. I'd been meaning to say good-bye to her, or at least try to explain things in a way she would understand, but because I didn't want to see Randy and because I couldn't bring myself to finalize anything, I'd never called. I wiped tears away from my eyes.

"Are you there, Monique?"

"I'm here, baby."

"Are you crying?"

I smiled and nodded my head. She was so perceptive. "Yes I am."

"Why? Did I do something?"

"No, no. Never, Jalisa. I'm crying because I'm happy. I've missed you so much."

Jalisa giggled, melting my heart. "Are you coming back home?"

"I don't know. I have to talk to your father."

"Daddy says you're mad at him. He says he did

the wrong things. I told him to do the right thing like you and Daddy always told me to do."

"Did he follow your advice?" I asked.

"I don't think so, because you're not here."

"Is your daddy there?"

There was a pause and then Jalisa said, "Yup."

"Can I speak to him?"

There was another pause, and this time I heard Jalisa whisper loudly, "She wants to speak to you." Then she put the receiver back to her mouth. "Yup. Monique, are you coming over?"

"I don't know, baby."

There was another pause as Jalisa consulted her adviser. "Can you come over?" she asked.

I smiled. Very clever.

"Let me talk to your father first."

"Pleeeeease? Pretty pleeeeeeeeease!"

I smiled and wiped more tears away. How could I have said no to an angel like that?

"Okay, I'll come over."

"Today?"

"Yup."

"Yaaay! She's coming, Daddy. She's coming!"

I couldn't help but laugh. "Put your daddy on for me now, honey."

"Okay. Bye. See you when you get here!"

I heard a muffling noise as Randy covered the phone with his palm. A few seconds later, he said, "Hey."

Goose bumps rose at the sound of his voice. It felt good to hear it live and not on a message.

"That was low, using Jalisa like that."

"I had no choice. I miss you."

I couldn't lie. "I miss you too."

"Did you get my messages?"

"All fifteen hundred of them."

"So you know that nothing happened between Tina and me?"

"That's what you say."

"It's the truth. I never asked for her to come over."

"Randy, I really don't want to go into that again."

"Jalisa wants to know what time you're coming over."

"Tell Jalisa I will be there at seven o'clock."

"She wants to know if you can make it eight?"

I smiled and wiped away a new wave of happy tears.

"Tell her eight o'clock will be fine."

I hung up the phone and went upstairs to get ready. I also packed an overnight bag.

Abe

After my bout with Taki I stopped at the flower shop on my way home and bought a bouquet of roses for Nakyia. I was feeling good. I'd saved my job and I'd shown Taki that she didn't have control over everything. I didn't mind that Brian now knew about my affair with her. He and I were in the same boat: we were men and we had needs. Besides, I had a feeling the "camaraderie" could help me out in the future. My meeting with him lasted for two hours. It took a half hour to go over my situation; the rest of the time was spent bull-shitting about women and golf. We had a lot more in common than I realized. We both had a weakness for fine women, we both loved Escalades, and someday when we grew up, we wanted to be just like Tiger Woods. I also found out that he didn't really respect Taki.

"She's a nice piece of scenery to look at, and it's cheaper than having a man in her position."

I pulled into the driveway, cut the engine and looked myself over in the mirror, checking for signs of Taki. Once I was satisfied that everything was cool, I grabbed the flowers and headed inside. Nakyia had been having a hard time with her neuralgia lately, and I wanted to try and do something to ease the stress from her mind. I wanted to take her out to eat, but I knew she wouldn't go for that. I figured a bouquet of long-stemmed red roses would help to bring a smile.

"Hey lady," I said, closing the door behind me. Nakyia was sitting on the couch on her laptop.

She looked up after a spasm of pain passed. "Hey yourself, handsome. Are those for me?"

I walked over to her and handed her the roses. "For my queen." I gave her a kiss on her forehead.

She put the laptop aside and got up from the couch, taking the roses into the kitchen. She came back a few seconds later and wrapped her arms around me and planted her lips on mine. I immediately pulled back.

"What are you doing? Are you trying to have another spasm of pain?"

"I've been having a good day," she said with a smile. "I miss kissing you. Don't hold back."

She pulled me back toward her and kissed me again, and I instantly became erect. If there was one thing that Nakyia never failed to do, it was excite me. I pulled her down to the floor and removed the T-shirt and shorts she was wearing. I paused for a moment to admire her body. She didn't go to the gym religiously like Taki did, but her body was no less spectacular. I traced her curves with my fingertips, making bumps rise from her skin. Nakyia moaned in a way I hadn't heard her in a long while. She began to touch herself as I caressed her breasts with my hands and tongue. I watched her performance and felt compelled to join her. After I removed my clothing, I did. We continued with our self-indulgence until Nakyia said, "Fuck me, Abraham."

Taking advantage of her good day, I did as she requested, and fucked her on the floor. I savored the feel of her beneath me as we moved in time to a muted melody. After a few minutes, Nakyia climbed on top of me and began to ride. Looking down at me, she whispered breathlessly, "Thrust harder."

I did.

"Push deeper!" she insisted.

I did.

"Fuck me faster!" she moaned.

I moved like the Tasmanian Devil on speed.

I followed her every command silently, and enjoyed the moment of uninhibited passion we shared. It had been too long since we had made love like that. I moaned along with her as goose bumps rose from my skin. We danced our dance until we both exploded, Nakyia first, and then me. When we were finished, we lay spent on the floor in each other's arms.

After a few minutes of satisfied silence, she said, "That was incredible."

"You were incredible."

"I want to make love like that all the time," she said softly.

"I wish we could."

"We'll be able to soon."

"What do you mean?"

Nakyia lifted her head and stared at me. "I'm

tired of having this nerve problem. I'm tired of the pain, tired taking the medicine. I'm tired of feeling like I'm not normal."

"Baby, you are normal."

"I don't feel like it, Abe. I can't do what the average person can do without having to suffer. I'm twenty-eight years old and I can't enjoy simple things like talking or eating. It's like I'm handicapped, only I don't have a sign."

"Baby, I know it's not easy, but what can you do? You can't stop taking the medication."

"Honey, I want to have the microvascular decompression procedure done."

"I thought we'd ruled that out."

"I know we discussed it, but I've been doing a lot of research on it. It's my only chance at having a normal life."

"But, Nakyia, what about the risks? You could lose hearing in your ear, the right side of your face could be numb forever, or worse, you could have a stroke and die."

"Honey, I know all about the risks and their probabilities, but that doesn't change my mind. I can't deal with this anymore. This nerve problem has disrupted my life in so many ways. Worst of all, it's disrupted us. I want to be able to make love like that all the time. But I want to be able to do it without wondering in the back of my head when the pain is going to hit me. I want to be able to go out with you again and not have to worry about how I look in public. I want you to not have to worry about holding back with me."

"Are you sure about this? I mean, for all intentional purposes, this is brain surgery we're talking about."

"I've already made my appointment and I have a plane ticket leaving for Pittsburgh, PA in three days to meet with the specialist to discuss when I can have the surgery done."

I nodded my head. "I'll get my ticket tomorrow."

Nakyia shook her head. "No. I want to go alone. Like they say, absence makes the heart grow fonder."

"True."

She gave me a kiss and rose from the floor and grabbed her clothing. "You know, after the surgery, life is going to change dramatically. It'll be a time to be happy again." She smiled and then headed upstairs.

I remained on the floor for a few minutes as I thought about the reality of her being without the disorder. My affair with Taki surfaced because of the neuralgia. Now, after experiencing some of the wildest and freakiest sex I'd ever had, would I be able to walk away from Taki and the convenience of having the one I loved at home and the one I fucked whenever I wanted? Although being with Taki was a risk and she did have feelings for me, I couldn't deny that I was hooked on what she was willing to give and do.

My train of thought was broken when Nakyia called out my name. She wanted seconds and I didn't mind obliging her at all. Today was certainly a good day. Maybe a lifetime of good days would be enough.

Randy

I didn't know what to expect with Monique after I finally got Jalisa to go to bed. The night had been perfect so far. Just like I'd hoped, Jalisa had kept a smile on Monique's face all night long. My little girl was genuinely thril-led to see her and before, during, and after dinner, and even on her way to bed, she filled Monique in on everything that had been going on in her pint-sized life. I didn't say much, but rather sat silent and watched the natural interaction between the two loves of my life. Using Jalisa to help me get Monique to come over had been a brilliant move. Too bad I hadn't thought of doing it sooner. Now that Jalisa was officially retired for the evening, I could only wonder what was going to happen next. I'd seen the overnight bag Monique had with her when she first arrived. I could only hope that it meant what I thought it meant.

"Well, it took a trip to Toys "R" Us, but she finally agreed to let me tuck her in," I said, coming back into the living room.

Sitting on the couch, Monique smiled. "I missed her. I didn't realize how much until tonight. I'm glad I came over."

After putting on a *Jazz by the Fireside* CD, I sat down beside her. "So does that mean that you're not mad at me?"

Monique looked at me. "Oh, I'm still mad at you. Don't get it twisted."

"Baby, I apologize for everything that's happened. I'm sorry about letting Tina interfere with our lives the way she did. I'm sorry that I never put her in her place the way I should have. I wanted to protect Jalisa, but I never stopped to realize that she never needed the protection. You were right—she could handle it."

"Oh, I know I was right. Randy, believe me, I admire what you were trying to do. I know that you meant well, but kids today don't need the protection like they used to. They're smarter than when we were kids and they're more grown. Unfortunately, kids growing up with estranged parents has become commonplace. Nowadays it's better for them to know and see the truth for what it is. Believe me—whether you showed it or not—Jalisa's always known that you and Tina can't get along."

I sighed. "Yeah, I know. Look Monique, I fucked up."

"Damn right you fucked up," she snapped. "I may have moved out, but this was still my home, and to know that you had that bitch in here doing God knows what . . ." She paused and squeezed her eyes tightly. I wanted to reassure her again that nothing happened, but kept silent. She opened her eyes and continued. "I wanted to slap the shit out of that bitch. Hell, I should have. I should have slapped you too. The only reason I didn't was because I didn't want to take the chance that Jalisa would be witness to anything. I didn't want to do that to her again."

"Monique, believe me, after all the calls I made to you, the last thing I wanted was for you to come and see that. I love you. All I want is for us to be back together again. I'm not the same without you. I don't have the same focus, the same desire. If Jalisa weren't here I would have jumped off of the Empire State Building by now."

"Oh, would you now?" Monique said with a smile.

I kept a straight face. "No. Make that the Eiffel Tower. The Empire State Building's not tall enough."

We shared a laugh and then got serious again. I looked at her with intense eyes. "Baby, I want you back where you belong."

"Where's that, Randy?"

"Here with me."

I kept my eyes locked on hers. Short of getting on my knees and reciting Babyface lyrics, I'd given it my best shot and didn't know what else to say. Monique didn't avert her gaze from mine as a saxophone crooned softly in the background.

"Randy," she finally said. "I'm going to be honest with you. I love you, and I do feel that my place is here with you. I want a future with you. But I don't want that if you don't have the balls to stand up to Tina. I don't deserve to be disrespected by her or any other bitch. Not in our home. Not anymore. Are you listening to what I'm saying? Do you understand what I'm getting at?"

I nodded my head and took her hand in mine. "Baby, I do understand. And I can assure you that things won't be the same. Tina knows what's up because I spoke to her."

"I don't want you to just speak to her, Randy! I want her ignorant ass to know her place."

I kissed Monique's knuckles and pulled her closer to me. She was reluctant at first, but eventually gave in. I kissed her gently on her forehead, and then I moved to her eyelids and nose, and finally worked my way down to her lips, where I paused. With my lips inches away from hers, I whispered, "I hope that bag you brought has your toothbrush."

Monique smiled and slit her eyes a fraction. "I guess you'll have to wait and find out."

We kissed again and then rose from the couch. That night we made slow, undying love. For the first time in a long while I didn't need to dream.

Abe

It was like déjà vu only this time it was in my office. It was after hours and I sat at my desk with Taki standing at the other side. She'd just told me all about what went down with her and her husband. I wanted to tell her that she was stupid for walking in her home with her underwear off, but I kept that thought to myself. I stared at the bruise from the slaps she'd gotten. I can't lie, if she were my wife, I'd probably have slapped her too.

"Well, with everything's that's happened, we really have no choice but to quit while we're ahead."

Taki put her hands on her waist. "Quit while we're ahead? What kind of an answer is that?"

"Look, Taki, you asked me what I think we should do, and that's what I think."

"But Whilice knows about us. We don't have to hide anymore."

I stood up and sighed. *Not again*, I thought. "Taki, we've gone over this before. There *is* no us. And you may be happy that Whilice knows, but I don't share the same sentiment. I'm not trying to have my spot blown."

"Don't worry about that. Whilice wouldn't say anything."

"How do you know he wouldn't?"

"Because he doesn't have the balls."

"He had the balls to hit you."

Taki didn't respond after my comment, and I could tell by the look on her face that Whilice's outburst had been a slap in the face for her both literally and physically.

"Look, Taki, Nakyia is going be having surgery to get rid of her nerve problem in a few weeks."

"So what does that mean?"

"Like I said, we need to quit what we have going on."

"Why? Because your wife is having surgery?"

"Things would have ended sooner or later, Taki."

"So your wife gets healed and my services are no longer needed. Is that how it works?"

"You said it, not me."

Taki shook her head. "You are a piece of shit, you know that? How the hell can you be so callous? Look at my face, Abe! Don't you even care at all about what happened to me? Aren't you worried about what more damage Whilice might do?"

"Look, I'm not trying to be cold. I'm just being real. You need to go home and try and diffuse the situation before it gets any worse."

"You mean before it gets any worse for you?"

I stared at her but kept silent.

"I don't know how the hell I could have ever fallen in love with such a bastard."

"You weren't supposed to fall in love."

"I hate you, Abe! You make me sick!"

"Whatever, Taki. Just remember you tried to fire me already."

Taki's eyes became slits as she said, "fuck you!" She stormed out of my office without another word.

I leaned back in my chair and massaged my temples. I'd played it cool in front of her, but the news about her husband had me worried. After Nakyia and I spoke about her decision to have the procedure, and especially after our lovemaking, I started to really believe that our marriage could get back to normal. We would be able to do all of the things we used to do. We could be the couple we were supposed to be, in love the way we were meant to be. I wanted my old life with Nakyia back, but now that Whilice knew the truth about Taki and me, I was worried that my old life could be jeopardized if it hadn't been already.

I picked up the phone to call my wife to see if Whilice had opened Pandora's box. My heart beat heavily as I waited for Nakyia to answer.

"Hello?"

"Hey sexy," I said slowly.

"Hey yourself, handsome. Are you coming home soon?"

"Yeah. I just called to see how you were."

"I'm doing fine. In pain as usual, but hopefully that will be over soon. I can't believe I'm having the procedure so soon. It normally takes a couple of months."

"I guess your time has come."

"Yeah."

"So other than the pain, nothing else happened today?" I asked, fishing.

"Nope."

"Good. Well, let me head out of here, then. I just wanted to say a quick hi and tell you I love you."

"I love you too."

I hung up the phone slightly relieved but no less concerned. What move would Whilice make, if any? And worse still, would I get any more grief from Taki?

Travis

With the rain pouring down around me and lightning crackling in the ugly gray clouds above, I hesitated for a brief second as I thought about how I ended up standing at the front door of Paul's home. Only his name wasn't Paul. I discovered that when I looked at his driver's license, and I can't tell you how much it hurt to know that what I thought had been his name was in fact his middle name. It meant that all the times he'd told me how special I was, and how much I'd meant to him, and what happiness I brought to his world, had all been a lie. The fact is if I were as special as he claimed I was, then I would have been calling him by the name everyone else used. That was truly the last straw for me. He could stay in the closet all he wanted, but he wasn't going to get another minute's worth of attention from me. I deserved better and would find better. I was done with him for good. But then I went to the doctor for my routine checkup, which I do every six months, and was given the worst news.

I was HIV positive.

I didn't want to believe it at first and had the test done over again. When the results came back the same, shock, anger, fear, and sadness hit me all at once. I went home and cried in my bed for days, barely eating and never sleeping.

HIV positive.

It was like being punished all over again.

I'd seen many friends die from the virus. I'd seen the pain and torment that their body and minds went through, and I promised myself that I would do all I could to keep the virus from turning me into another sad statistic.

AIDS.

The word kept hitting me over and over, beating at me, begging me to let it come inside.

Once my tear ducts ran dry, I sat and thought about all of the partners I'd been with without wearing protection. I could only come up with two people. The first time I'd gone bareback had been with Bill back when I was sixteen, so I eliminated him from the picture. My second time had been with Paul—well, not Paul anymore. We only had sex once without a condom, and that was because he said that he wanted to feel me raw inside of him. I was reluctant to at first, but when he started to go on and on about how much I meant to him and how we didn't need the barrier in-between us, I gave in.

Now here I was.

I pressed the doorbell, took a deep breath, and shivered from the chill of the downpour. The umbrella that I had bought at the airport wasn't the greatest, and rain was still getting to me. I was about to press the doorbell again when I looked up and saw a pair of eyes appear in-between the curtain by the window to the side. I knew whose eyes they were. They lingered for a second and then disappeared. Five minutes later, the front door opened.

"What the fuck are you doing here?"

"Hello to you too, Paul," I said evenly. "Or should I say, Brian? After all, that is your first name that you never bothered to give me."

Brian glared back at me and in another raging whisper said, "What the fuck are you doing here, Travis?"

"We need to talk."

Brian took a quick glance behind him and then stepped outside and closed the door. I looked him up and down for a second and then shook my head.

"Travis, you need to leave. Now."

"I'm not going anywhere until we talk."

Brian took a step toward me, not caring that he was getting wet and pushed me back. "We don't have anything to talk about, Travis. Now I'm telling you for the last time, get the fuck away from my home."

"I tested positive, Brian," I said bluntly.

Thunder exploded in the sky above as Brian said, "What?"

"I'm HIV positive. You gave me AIDS, you asshole!"

I didn't mean to come off that way, but with the heavy rain, the thunder and lightning, and Brian standing before me as if he were better than me, I found myself unable to contain my anger. He'd handed me a death sentence and he was going to get a piece of my mind.

"What the fuck are you talking about, Travis? What do you mean, you're HIV positive?"

I pointed my index finger straight at him. "I mean that your trifling, diseased ass gave me AIDS."

Brian shook his head. "You're lying."

"I figured you'd say that." I dug into my pants pocket. "Here are the test results." I held up a folded piece of paper for him to take. Brian looked at my outstretched hand and then up at me. "Take it and see if I'm lying, Brian."

Brian smirked and folded his arms across his chest. He looked at the piece of paper in my hand again. I could tell that he was worried. "Take it, damn it!"

Brian clenched his jaws and then grabbed the paper from my hand. "This is a stupid game to play, Travis," he said, opening the paper. I stood silent for a tense five seconds as he scanned the results, and then suddenly, before I even knew what was happening, Brian viciously hit me in the face. I fell back to the wet pavement, dropping my umbrella. I knew immediately that my nose had been broken.

"You fucking liar!" Brian raged. "That's a fucking lie! I don't have any goddamned AIDS, you pathetic homo."

As I lay on the ground dazed while my HIV-infected blood gushed from my nose and mixed with the falling rain, the front door opened behind Brian.

"Oh my God! What the hell is going on?"

Brian turned around quickly. "Natalie, go back inside," he ordered.

Natalie stared at me with wide-eyed confusion as I struggled to my feet.

"Brian, what is going on? Why are you fighting? Who is that?" She looked at me. "Who are you?"

"Go back inside, Natalie," Brian demanded again, trying to usher her back into the house. I staggered over to my test results, now soaked, and picked it up.

"I'm sure I don't need to ask, but are you his wife?" I was feeling dizzy from the blow I'd received; surely one of his best.

"Yes, but who—"

"Go back inside!" Brian yelled, cutting her off. He turned to me. "Travis, I'm giving you one last fucking chance to get the fuck out of here!"

"Or what, Brian? You'll beat me up again like all of the other times?"

"What's he talking about, Brian?" Natalie asked. Through the rain, I could see the confusion in her eyes thickening.

Brian faced his wife again. "He's not talking about anything. Now go back inside and let me deal with him."

"Oh, I'm not?" I looked at his wife. "There's something that you need to know about your husband."

Turning back around toward me, Brian yelled, "Shut the fuck up, Travis!"

I ignored him and kept my eyes locked on Natalie's. "He loves it when I suck his dick."

I laughed as blood flowed and a wave of dizziness and pain hit me. I didn't intend on being so vulgar but I was pissed.

Pissed at Brian for hurting me physically and emotionally.

Pissed at his wife for having the top spot.

Pissed at myself for not using protection.

I came to confront Brian, not hurt his wife, but now I didn't care. "I'm Brian's lover, Natalie. And believe me—he enjoys getting it up the ass a hell of a lot more than you do."

"Shut up, Travis!" Brian yelled. He turned back to Natalie, who was shaking her head. "Baby, don't listen to him. He's lying."

"If I'm lying, why do I have your wallet?" I asked, removing it from my other pocket and throwing it at him.

Natalie picked it up from the ground and gripping it tightly, shoved it into Brian's face. "You told me you lost this!"

"Baby . . . I did."

"Then why does he have it?" She pointed at me as tears leaked from her eyes. I was completely drenched now, but didn't care or notice. "Why does he have your wallet, Brian?"

"Baby, I don't know how he got it."

"Oh, please," I said. "You know damn well you left it at my place in New York."

"New York?" Natalie asked.

I nodded. "Oh, yes. That's where I live, and that's where he stays for a little rest and relaxation, because it's tough being cramped inside of that closet. Isn't it, Brian?"

"No!" Natalie yelled out. "Brian . . . please, no!"

"Baby, he's lying," Brian insisted. "I swear to you." He turned away from her and faced me. "Tell her you're lying, Travis! Tell her now!"

"I'm not telling her anything but the truth!" I yelled back defiantly. "You are a homosexual. I am your partner. And you gave me AIDS!"

As if on cue, lighting snapped and lit up the gray sky. Natalie cried out again. "Please, no! Please, Brian! No! No! No!"

"Baby . . . it's not true," Brian insisted.

"Look me in the eye and tell me he's lying," Natalie demanded.

"He's fucking lying," Brian said, still trying to beat me down with his gaze.

Natalie grabbed him by the shoulders and spun him around. "Look at me, damn it! Not him!"

Brian stared at her but didn't say anything.

"Tell me, Goddamnit!"

I watched Brian shake his head.

"I love you, Natalie," he said, attempting to hug her, but she pushed him away.

"That's not what I want to hear!"

"Baby . . ."

"Are you gay?"

"Baby . . ."

"Is he your lover? Do you have AIDS? Oh God, do I?"

"Tell her, Brian," I cut in. "Tell her what we do in the bedroom."

"Shut the fuck up!" Brian raged with his back to me and Natalie eyeing him.

I kept going. "Tell her about the special toys we use. Tell her about your favorite positions. Tell her what character you like to play."

Still, with his back to me, "Travis, shut the fuck up!"

"Tell me, Brian!" Natalie insisted.

"Tell her Brian!"

"Travis, if you don't shut up I swear I'm going to kill you!"

"What, you're not going to just beat me up, Brian? You're going to kill me now?" My heart was beating heavily like the angry raindrops falling down around us. I had the feeling that something terrible was about to happen. There was an ill feeling in the breeze around us. An eerie gasp that wouldn't subside. I know I should have stopped pushing buttons. I should have quit while I was ahead. But I just couldn't. For the first time I felt like I was the one coming out on top. I was the victor and my spoils were Brian's embarrassment and fear.

"Is that what you want to do, Brian? Kill me?"

I was about to say something else, but before I could, Brian spun around, removed a gun hidden in his waistline, pointed the muzzle at my chest and squeezed the trigger. I felt like I'd been hit with a thousand-pound sledgehammer as I fell to the ground seconds after the blast.

"I told you to leave!" I heard Brian say above Natalie's screaming. Of course, all of this seemed so far away as my chest burned and blood leaked from my chest wound, making me warm and then cold all at the same time.

"I told you to fucking leave!" I heard Brian say again.

Then Natalie: "Oh my God! Brian . . . What have you done!"

"You . . . you shot me," I said faintly. "You shot me," I lifted my head and tried to rise, but the pain was too severe. Suddenly, everything around me began to spin frantically, forcing me to lay my head back onto the wet, hard ground.

He'd shot me.

As Natalie screamed, I looked past the falling rain to the gray clouds above, only they didn't seem so gray anymore. I coughed harshly and when I did, I spit up blood.

Brian had shot me, and I was dying.

I thought about the way my life began at the age of sixteen when I came out of hiding, and compared it to how it was now ending. I don't think I've ever been happier or more relieved than these two moments in my time. I said a prayer for my mother and Randy and thanked them for all they'd done for me. I also said a prayer for my father and Abe, and asked God not to punish them for being who they were. I think I smiled as I closed my eyes and prepared to move on to my next life. I just hoped that I would never take the last conversation I'd ever hear with me.

"Brian . . . What have you done?"

"I told him to leave! I gave him a chance!"

"Oh my God! Oh God!"

"I don't have AIDS. I can't have AIDS."

"Brian, put the gun down. Please!"

"It's not true. I don't have AIDS."

"Brian . . . please put the gun down."

"Natalie . . . I'm so sorry . . . I'm so sorry. I never meant for this to happen. I love you."

"I love you too, Brian. Now please put the gun down!"

"Don't tell the boys the truth. Tell them I was arguing about money. Tell them anything . . . just don't tell them the truth."

"You can tell them you had a fight yourself, Brian. Please put the gun down!"

"I love them, Natalie. I love them. They look up to me. Please don't tell them. Let me be the man in their eyes."

"Tell them you love them later, Brian."

"I'm so sorry. So sorry. I love you. God forgive me."

Bang.

"Briannnnn!!!!!"

That was the last thing I ever heard. Please God, I begged as my life ended, don't let that conversation come with me.

Randy

Monique was in my arms crying softly, while I sat stoic and in shock. Travis was dead. Shot and killed by his lover.

I'd gotten the call from Officer Frank Krebbs from the Miami police department, because I was listed as Travis's emergency contact. He told me with little to no emotion, although his voiced was laced with a *he got what he deserved* tone. Travis was dead and he was HIV positive. Though he probably didn't want to, the officer told me how it all went down, as told to him by Brian's wife.

"Apparently, your brother found out that he was HIV positive and went to confront Mr. Wilson. As you've probably guessed by now, Mr. Wilson was in the closet about his . . . ah . . . preference, which is a damn shame really, considering the fact that Mrs. Wilson is such a beautiful woman. Most guys only wish to have someone that attractive. I'll never understand how a man could go for another man. It's just not natural. I mean—"

"Just tell me the rest of the story, Officer," I said, cutting him off.

"Ah yeah. Anyway, your brother went to confront him and when he did, they started arguing. Mrs. Wilson became involved after her husband had already broken your brother's nose. Ha ha. I didn't even know they could fight. Anyway, after a whole bunch of shouting, Mr. Wilson pulled a gun from his waistband and pulled the trigger, killing your brother. Then he turned it on himself."

I took a deep breath and released it slowly. Monique and I were supposed to have been making love. Jalisa was visiting my mother, and the plan was to take advantage of the alone time. When the call came through, Monique told me to let the call go to the answering machine, but just in case it was Jalisa, I hadn't. Now I almost wished I had.

I told her what had been told to me, and as her tears fell from her eyes I stared blankly with my hands balled tightly.

Damn Travis.

I took another deep breath, closed and squeezed my eyes tightly, and massaged my temples. I'd finally managed to get the stress from Tina off my back, and now I had to deal with this.

"I have to call my mom," I said quietly. "I have to tell her what happened."

Monique sniffled and looked up at me through swollen, red eyes. "Are you okay?"

I shrugged my shoulders. "I don't know," I answered honestly. "I guess I always knew that a call like this could come, especially given the lifestyle he'd lived, but it was always just a thought. This is real. My little brother is dead."

"I'm sorry, baby."

"I want to shed tears, but for some reason I can't. And I don't know why. Maybe I'm too angry to cry. Why couldn't he have just taken my advice? Why did he have to keep going back to him?"

Rubbing my shoulders, Monique said, "Baby, he was an adult. He had to do what made him happy."

"So being somebody's punching bag made him happy?"

"Baby, that was his choice."

"Some choice," I snapped. I stood up and walked to our dressing table and stared at my reflection in the glass; Travis stared back at me. "Why did he have to be gay, Monique? I mean, he grew up in the same house as Abe and I did. He saw how our parents interacted with one another. Why did he decide to be gay? No one ever showed him that."

"Randy, you know that it wasn't his choice. That's how he was born."

I gritted my teeth. "How could it not have been his choice? We all have a choice."

"Randy, why are you talking like Abe? You know that Travis was gay since he was a child. He didn't choose anything. It's just who he was."

"Then why couldn't he have been someone else?" I asked, pounding my fist on the top of the dresser.

"Baby, if he would have been, then there'd be no Travis."

"Yeah well, being Travis got him killed."

"Randy, you know that isn't true. His being gay

is not what got him killed. I'm surprised that you would even say that."

I turned and looked at Monique. "It wasn't?"

Monique stood and approached me. "No, it wasn't. Travis fell in love, plain and simple. His choice of partners got him killed."

My shoulders slumped as Monique's words, which I knew were true, sunk in. "Why couldn't he have just taken my advice?" I asked again, a lump rising in my throat. "Why didn't he listen?"

Monique reached out and took me in her arms as tears of anger, regret, and grief erupted from my eyes.

Her hand going around in slow circles on my back, Monique said, "Baby, he had his path to follow."

Unable to reply, I just wrapped my arms around her and let out my pain. A few minutes later, I lifted my head from Monique's shoulder and looked at her. "I love you," I said.

"I love you back." She kissed me softly. "Make your calls, baby."

I inhaled deeply and let out the air slowly and nodded. "I'm worried about how my mother's going to take the news."

"Randy, your mother is a strong woman. She'll be okay."

We kissed again and then I moved to the phone. As I reluctantly pressed the buttons for my mother's number, Monique, who was walking out of the bedroom, said, "Randy, promise me that you'll call Abe and tell him what happened."

"What for? To hear the pleasure in his voice?"

"Travis was his brother too, whether he liked it or not. He has a right to know."

"He won't care."

"Promise me."

"It will fall on deaf ears."

"Promise me," she insisted with her hands on her hips.

I sighed. "I promise."

Monique gave me a half-smile and left the room. I finished dialing my mother's phone number. When she answered, I didn't bother beating around the bush. "Ma, Travis is dead."

Silence answered me, and then ten seconds later my mother said, "Sweet Jesus. It was Paul, wasn't it?"

"Yes it was."

"I always knew he would be the death of my boy. How did it happen?"

"He shot him," I said evenly.

"Lord," my mother whispered.

I continued with my straightforwardness. "He gave Travis HIV, and Travis went to confront him about it. Paul, whose first name is actually Brian, was married and his wife was there when he killed Travis and eventually shot himself."

"Sweet Jesus. He gave my boy HIV and he was married . . . That poor woman."

"I have to go and identify Travis's body, Ma. I'll be flying to Florida today."

"Florida? What's his body doing there?"

"That's where Brian lived."

"Did you tell your brother yet?"

"No."

"Make sure you do."

"I will. Are you going to tell Dad?"

"Of course. Why wouldn't I?"

"Because he wouldn't care."

"Well, whether he wants to accept it or not, Travis was his son."

Was.

That was a hard word to hear.

I was silent for a few seconds and then said, "I can't believe he's dead, Ma."

"It . . . it was his time to go, baby," my mother responded, her voice quivering as she began to cry softly.

"I'm going to call Abe."

"Okay."

"Do you want me to buy you a plane ticket?"

Silence again took over and as I sat waiting for my mother's response, I listened to her break down and sob. It hurt my heart to tell her that her youngest son, my baby brother, was dead.

"Randy," my mother said after a few minutes passed. "You go without me, okay?"

"Okay, Ma. I'll call when I get back. And do me a favor and don't tell Jalisa, okay. I'll tell her when I come home."

"Okay, baby."

I was about to hang up when my mother called me. "Yeah, Ma?"

"I have a favor to ask also."

"What's that?"

"Stop by Brian's home and pay your respect to his wife. Travis did her wrong, and she needs an apology."

"Do you really think that would be a good idea?"

"Baby, Travis's actions have changed her life forever. It's the least that we can do."

"Okay, Ma. I will."

"Thank you, baby."

I hung up the phone without saying good-bye, because it just seemed inappropriate. I waited about a half hour before I called Abe. I just needed some time to sit and digest what had happened. I never had the time to let the fact that Travis was messing around with a married man sink in. My mother was right. Travis's selfishness did change Brian's wife's world forever. I couldn't even begin to imagine the betrayal, anger, and pain that she must have been feeling. I sighed and closed my eyes. My brother and a married man; he was a mistress. It was an odd thing to think.

I shook my head and picked up the phone again. Calling Abe was not something I was looking forward to, because there was no doubt in my mind that Travis's death would do nothing more than please him, and that pissed me off, which was not a good thing considering the fact that I knew we were going to get into a heated argument. It was something that couldn't be avoided, though. Not when the subject was Travis. I just hoped that the argument wouldn't escalate into something ugly and full of regret. Unfortunately, as I dialed his number, I had a feeling that things between us would never be the same.

"Hello?"

"Abe, it's Randy."

"Hey, what's up, big brother? How are things

going on the home front? You finally put Tina in check?"

"Abe, Travis is dead," I said, getting straight to the point.

There was a slight moment of silence before Abe said, "So how's my niece doing?"

"Abe, did you just hear what I said? Travis was shot and killed."

"So what the hell are you telling me for?" Abe asked angrily.

I stood up, no longer able to stay seated, and paced around my bedroom. "What do you mean, why am I telling you? Travis was your brother."

"Randy, how many times do I have to tell you that faggot was not my brother."

"Goddamn, Abe!" I yelled.

"Goddamn, Abe, what?" my brother yelled back. "What, you want me to actually give a shit that the homo is dead? You want me to shed tears and lose sleep? Fuck that! I said it years ago, I said it two minutes ago, and I'll say it now . . . that faggot was not my brother! I don't know why you constantly waste your breath and my time by talking to me about him. So he's dead. So the fuck what! He probably deserved what he got."

I kicked the hell out of my bedroom door, putting a hole in it, as I had reached the boiling point. "You are a fucking piece of shit, Abe. How the fuck can you disrespect your own flesh and blood like that? How can you say that your own baby brother deserved to die?"

"Shut the fuck up with that bullshit you're spitting, Randy. Live or die, I don't give a shit about Travis's ass."

"So it's like that?" I asked, seething.

"It's been like that," Abe responded callously.

I shook my head and pounded my fist against the wall. "I can't believe you are that selfish, man. He was your brother. Fuck his lifestyle. It was his, not yours."

"Yeah, well, he could have that."

"What the fuck were you so afraid of, man, that you disowned your own blood? What the hell are you so afraid of now that you can't pay him any respect in his death? Are you not comfortable with yourself? Was Travis being gay hitting a little too close to home for you? Do you have secrets that you're trying to hide?"

"Fuck you, Randy!"

I snapped back. "No, fuck you, Abe, and your insecurities and your selfishness! You want to be a goddamned homophobic bitch, you go ahead. You can be an ass all you want."

"So what are you saying?" Abe asked.

"I'm saying that I've had it with your shit. Travis is dead, man, and all you can do is stand over his grave and smile. You are a true piece of work, and you know what, since it was so easy to forget about Travis, you can forget about me too."

I slammed the phone down, without waiting for a response from him, and threw the phone against the wall, causing it to shatter. Monique, who'd been standing by the bedroom door the whole time, walked up behind me and wrapped her arms around my waist. I didn't say a word as she kissed me softly on the back of my neck. I was breathing heavily. I bit down on my bottom lip and exhaled loudly. Frustration, rage, and sadness oozed from

my pores, and I still had the trip to Florida to
make. I looked at the hole I'd made and the
phone I'd broken. The broken mess could have
just as easily been Abe. Brother or no brother, he
was lucky that we had states in-between us, because
had we been in the same room, I wouldn't have
hesitated to give him a beat down. I leaned my
head back and took a moment to enjoy Monique's
tender pecks. I knew that would be my only moment of peace for a while.

Abe

I slammed the phone down and looked away from Nakyia, who'd been sitting silent, glaring at me during my entire conversation with Randy.

"Are you really that selfish?" she asked in a disgusted tone.

I groaned. "Nakyia, don't start anything with me, okay. I'm not in the mood."

Nakyia stood up, rested her hands on her hips, and curled her lips into an ugly snarl. "I don't care what you're in the mood for, Abe. Your brother is dead. How could you disrespect him the way you just did?"

I clasped my hands above my head. "Jesus Christ! How many times do I have to say that I don't give a damn about Travis? I don't care that he's dead. He meant nothing to me!"

"He was your brother! His being gay shouldn't have made him anything less than that."

"It did in my book," I said bluntly.

"That's really narrow-minded. His being gay had nothing to do with the type of person that he was.

His sexuality didn't make him any less of a person. What he did in the bedroom wasn't any business of yours, and it really sucks that you can't look past that now to pay him some damned respect. He was your brother!"

"I am so tired of hearing everyone talk about respecting Travis!" I yelled out. "Was he respecting our father when he announced that he was gay?" I didn't wait for an answer. "No, he wasn't. My father felt like a failure because of him."

"Oh, please, Abe. Travis's coming out had nothing to do with what your father did or didn't do."

"Nakyia, Travis's lifestyle was a damn sin. Doesn't that matter? Doesn't it matter that he brought shame to the whole family?"

"Get it right, Abe. He brought shame to you and your father."

"Whatever. Look, let's just end this now. Travis is dead and life goes on. I'm not wasting any more time, and I'm certainly not wasting any tears on him."

"Is it really that simple?"

"Yes it is," I answered honestly. "What are you so upset for, anyway? You never even met him. Why the hell should you care if he lived or died?"

"I care because he was your family. And that made him mine. I'm upset because your ignorance kept both of us from getting to know someone that we could have loved. He was a man, Abe. A gay man. A human being. You better hope and pray that when your time comes God doesn't judge you the way you've judged Travis all these years."

"Whatever, Nakyia. Like I said, in the Bible

Travis's lifestyle was a sin. If anyone should worry at the pearly gates, it should be him."

Nakyia slit her eyes at me. "Go to hell, Abe." She stormed out of the living room angrily without another word.

I sat down on my sofa and closed my eyes. My head was beginning to throb. I needed aspirin. I was about to get up and get some when Nakyia came back into the living room with her car keys and purse in hand.

"Where are you going?" I asked.

"To get the hell away from you," she said irritably. "But before I go, I just wanted to say that I have no doubt in my mind that you will never be half the man that I'm sure Travis was."

Before I could respond to her comment, Nakyia walked out the door, got in her car, and drove off. It was a good thing she did, because nothing but ugliness was going to come from my mouth. I cursed out loud and went to the kitchen and grabbed a beer. I was heated. The argument with Randy, the argument with Nakyia; why the hell couldn't Travis have been the brother that he was supposed to?

I cursed out loud, downed the beer as if I hadn't had anything to drink for days and then grabbed another one. My hands were shaking I was so angry.

I was halfway through my second beer when my cell phone went off. I picked it up from the counter and looked at the caller ID. For the first time in a long while I was actually happy to see Taki's number displayed on the fluorescent green screen, because the only time she called my cell was when she wanted some, which didn't bother me because I was in dire need of some hardcore fucking at that moment. With Taki going through her own drama at home, there was no doubt in my mind that hardcore would be her pleasure for the day. I hit my talk button.

"What's up, Taki?"

"Abe . . . did . . ." Taki paused and sniffled. I could tell that she was crying. Immediately I thought about Whilice, and wondered if he had hit her again.

"What's wrong, Taki? Are you okay?"

Taki sniffed again. "Did you hear the news about Brian?"

"What news?"

Another sniffle. "Bri—Brian's dead."

"What?" I asked, leaning against the kitchen counter. "What do you mean, he's dead?"

"He . . . shot himself yesterday," she said in a whisper.

"Come on, Taki, Brian wouldn't do something like that. Who told you that? Someone's playing a cruel joke on you."

"It's no joke, Abe. It was on the news last night. Brian shot and killed himself after . . . after . . ." she paused again, leaving me hanging in shock.

"After what, Taki?"

"Abe . . . Brian was gay. He shot and killed his lover in front of his home, with Natalie there."

I nearly fell, as my legs became rubber. Gay? Brian was gay? "What do you mean, he was gay? What do you mean, he shot his lover? Taki, this shit isn't funny."

"I'm not joking!" Taki yelled. "It was on the

news. Brian was gay and his lover came to confront him. Brian shot him and then turned the gun on himself."

I shook my head. I couldn't believe it. Not Brian. Not the man with the raging temper on the golf course. He couldn't have been. I thought about the times I met Brian and a few other guys from work for happy-hour drinks. We'd all sit around and crack jokes, and stare at women.

No way.

Brian was a man's man.

A cigar-smoking, beer-drinking, sport-loving man.

"Taki . . . there's just no way," I said, still denying it. "Absolutely no way."

"Abe, it's true. I saw it on the news today. I even drove by his house to see if they were talking about the same Brian. There are candles and crosses sitting in his front lawn, Abe."

I shook my head again. Gay. Brian was gay.

And then a terrible thought hit me with the force of a cannonball. I took a slow, deep breath and let it out painfully slow as I spoke into the phone. "Taki . . . he . . . the person Brian shot . . . Did they release his name?" I clenched my jaws and waited for an answer that I prayed would not be the one I suspected.

Taki sniffled. "I . . . I think his name was Trevor or Travis. Something like that. Why?"

The phone fell from my hand before I could even think to answer her.

Travis. Dead. Shot and killed.

Brian. Gay. Shot and killed his lover.

It had to be a coincidence. A cruel, sick, unbe-

lievable coincidence. I stumbled out of the
kitchen, leaving my cell phone on the floor. I
think I faintly heard Taki yelling out my name as I
reached for the phone in the living room. My
hands shook as I dialed Randy's phone number.

Brian was gay. Brian was gay. The sentence kept
repeating in my mind over and over like a scratch
on a CD.

"What do you want, Abe?" Randy said, answering the phone angrily.

I took a deep breath. "Who was the person that
killed Travis?" My heart was racing as though I'd
just done an hour's worth of cardio as I waited for
Randy's answer.

"What the hell do you want to know for?"

"I need to know, Randy," I said my voice and
hands trembling. "I need to know."

"You need to know? What do you care?"

"Look, just tell me, okay." I could feel myself
ticking, about to go off.

"Why?"

I snapped. "Goddamn it, Randy! Just answer the
fucking question! Who the fuck killed Travis? Was
it someone named Brian? That's all I want to
know. Was it someone named Brian?" I squeezed
my eyes shut and gritted my teeth.

"Why the hell are you asking me if you already
know the answer, Abe?"

I never answered my brother. Instead I threw
the phone across the room and cursed out loud as
it shattered against the wall. I yelled out loud again
and swung out at a table lamp, sending it shatter-
ing on the ground. I staggered as my entire body
felt as though I were burning inside.

Travis and Brian.

Brian and Travis.

That combination spun around and around, blurring my vision, making my knees weaker and weaker.

Travis and Brian.

Brian and Travis.

Then I blacked out.

Randy

Sitting on the relatively quiet plane ride to Florida, I reflected on life without Travis to watch out for. Although we never had the normal sibling relationship that I would have preferred, we'd had a relationship nonetheless. If there was one thing I could rely on, it was that I could always count on Travis calling on me to pick him up and dust him off whenever he'd fallen. That was the brotherly relationship we'd developed, and I'd come to depend on that role. I'm pretty sure Travis had become dependent on my role too. I never hesitated to be there even when he'd put himself in certain predicaments he had no right being in. But that was Travis, and I loved him despite of it.

I sighed. I still didn't want to believe that he was dead. I balled my fists tightly as I thought about how final death was. I balled them even tighter as my thoughts switched to Abe. I was still burning inside over our argument. His anger toward Travis I could always deal with, but his refusal to pay Travis respect in death was something that disgusted me. That he was filled with so much rage and hatred toward his own blood was disturbing. As far as I was concerned, he had practically squeezed the trigger along with Brian. I couldn't help but wonder what kind of man my brother actually was.

I used to wonder what he would do, or how he would react if he and Nakyia ever found themselves in the same situation as our parents. Would love and understanding have ever been able to find a way into his heart? Or would hatred and intolerance have blackened it for good? Well, I could stop wondering because I knew for sure that he would disown his own child just as our father had done.

I stretched and looked at two little boys sitting beside me. They were brothers lost in their Game Boy Advance world, playing Mortal Kombat. I was never any good at video games. I never had the patience required to master them. Not like Abe, who had been the Nintendo guru of the neighborhood. Travis, of course, was never into the games, although he did like to watch occasionally.

I watched the brothers play their games and wondered if either one of them would grow up to be like Travis or Abe. I sighed and thought about how in one day I'd lost both of my brothers. I wanted to tell the youngsters to always love each other no matter what. That they were blood and there was nothing more important than that. One of the boys looked up at me suddenly, as if he'd heard my thoughts, and gave me a smile. I smiled back and then closed my eyes and slept the rest of the trip.

After arriving in Florida, I checked into a hotel and then reluctantly went to the morgue. When I got there I wanted to turn right around and head back home. I didn't want to walk through the doors, and I didn't want to announce to anyone that I was there to identify my brother's body. I didn't want to walk into the cold room that smelled like sweetened mold, filled with soulless cadavers, covered by white sheets, laying on steel gurneys. Telling the balding white gentleman, with eyes magnified by lenses as thick as Coke bottles and teeth the color of faded gold, who looked like he enjoyed his job just a little too much, to go ahead and lift the sheet for me to say that the graying body did indeed belong to Travis, was not what I wanted to do at all. But that's just what I did. And afterward I threw up what little I'd somehow managed to eat and anything else that was left over.

After filling out whatever paperwork I needed to, I took Travis's belongings and went back to the hotel. Before my mother asked me to go and see Brian's wife, I'd planned on going straight back to New York. I didn't want to stay in Florida any longer than I needed to. Now I had no choice. I stood in the shower while hot water cascaded down over my shoulders and cried softly as images of Travis laying lifeless on the gurney passed painstakingly through my mind.

Monique

It was mid-morning and I was just starting to dream when the phone rang. I had taken the day off to make an attempt at catching up on the sleep that I'd lost after getting the news about Travis. I decided to play hooky after making sure that Jalisa had gotten to school on time. I was physically and mentally drained and the thought of going to work just wasn't agreeing with me.

When I got home, I straightened up and sat on the couch watching one of Jalisa's favorite cartoons, which were fast becoming a favorite of mine. It was amazing how easily I'd transitioned into the role of motherhood. The more I did with Jalisa, the more I wanted to have a child of my own. I mean, don't get me wrong, I loved taking care of Jalisa, and at times I really did feel like a mother, but no matter what I did or how much of an influence I had, I knew that Tina would always be Mommy and I would always be Monique—the stepmother. Since Randy and I had gotten back on the track, my desire to experience the entire process of motherhood only grew stronger. I wanted to know what it was like to have a child growing inside of me, despite the horror stories some of my girlfriends told me about morning sickness, fatigue, hormonal changes, and weight gain. I wanted to watch my belly rise with motion from my child. I wanted to have the sonograms to stare at and wonder what features of mine and Randy's he or she would have. I promised myself that after the tragedy over Travis had passed, I was going to sit down and have a talk with Randy about my feelings.

When the cartoons ended, I sought the warmth and comfort of my bed. I was just starting to dream about babies when the call came. I rose from the bed like an old woman and grabbed the phone. "Hello?"

"Good morning, is Mr. Randy Lincoln available?"

Groggily, I said, "No, he's not."

"Well, is Ms. Monique Jones there?"

My eyes opened a notch wider. "Speaking. Who's calling?"

"Ms. Jones, my name is Eduardo Sanchez. I'm the guidance counselor at P.S. One-thirty-nine. I'm calling about Jalisa."

I sat up. "Is she all right? Is she hurt?"

"Jalisa's fine, Ms. Jones. She's in class right now as we speak."

I breathed a sigh of relief. "So what can I do for you, Mr. Sanchez?"

"Well, I'm a little concerned about Jalisa's

behavior and since you are listed as her secondary point of contact, I'm hoping that you could come down to the school for a private meeting."

"Of course. I can be there in about twenty minutes."

"That would be perfect."

"Ms. Jones, it's a pleasure to meet you."

I shook Mr. Sanchez's hand and sat down in a chair opposite his desk. His office was tiny but comfortable with his desk, a small sofa, and beige carpeting. On his wall he had his college degree, numerous certifications, and a small flag of Puerto Rico. I looked at the couple of photographs of his family sitting on his desk and smiled. "Your wife is very beautiful, and your two boys are going to be dangerous when they get older."

Mr. Sanchez smiled proudly. "Thank you. That's Anthony on the right and Maxwell on the left. And trust me, my wife and I call them little devils already. They are a handful."

I smiled and felt my skin rise with goose bumps. I was definitely going to have that talk with Randy.

"So what's the problem with Jalisa?"

"Well, during the past couple of weeks, Jalisa's behavior has been unusual, and I'm just a little concerned."

"Unusual? What do you mean?"

"Jalisa is one of our brightest and most energetic students. She gets along well with all of her peers as well as the teachers. But lately she just hasn't been herself. She's been very detached, often keeping to herself during recess and lunch, and not participating during class like she normally does. The teachers have also noticed that she's been doodling and daydreaming more. As I said, this behavior is unusual for her, and I'm just wondering if there could be any problems going on at home that may be affecting her? A loss of a pet, a death of a loved one? Family problems, perhaps?"

I shook my head. "No. Everything at home is fine. Her father and I had gone through a rough period a few weeks ago, but that's been resolved. I have to be honest, I haven't noticed anything but Jalisa being her usual self. Are you sure that she's not having a problem with one of the kids here at school?"

"We did wonder about that, but as far as we can tell, that's not an issue. What is Jalisa's relationship like with her mother?"

"She and her mother get along just fine. Her mother is a fashion model, and because she's always doing photo shoots, Jalisa only gets to see her four months out of the year."

"And what is your relationship with her mother?"

"We . . . tolerate each other."

"So then you two are at odds?"

"In a word, yes. We don't get along too well. Her mother is not very supportive of my relationship with Jalisa's father."

Mr. Sanchez nodded his head slowly and scribbled something into a pad he had placed before him. "That's what I figured. Let me show you something." He reached into one of his desk drawers and removed a small manila folder. From it he removed a yellow piece of construction paper and handed it to me. "During art class yesterday Jalisa drew this picture. The assignment was for them to draw a picture of their family."

I took the paper and opened it, and sighed. Jalissa had drawn a picture of a couple holding hands, while a little girl stood in front of them crying. The reason for her tears was to the right of the little girl—a tall woman with red horns and fangs. The picture was a sad depiction of the pain Tina's crap had brought to Jalisa's world.

"Based on what you told me," Mr. Sanchez said, "I'm going to assume that you and Mr. Lincoln are the couple holding hands, and the woman with the horns is Jalisa's mother."

I nodded. "Yes, this picture fits her to a T."

"Out of curiosity, Ms. Jones, do you share that type of sentiment with Jalisa?"

I shook my head. "No. I keep my thoughts and feelings to myself and Randy. I may not have a friendly relationship with her mother, but I know not to project my ill feelings about her onto Jalisa. It's hard sometimes, but I respect the fact that Tina is her mother. But believe me, Mr. Sanchez, I really don't have to say anything negative, because Tina does that with her actions."

Mr. Sanchez nodded and scribbled into his pad again. "I'm glad that you've taken the position you have. Oftentimes, adults don't do that. Perhaps you and Mr. Lincoln could speak to Jalisa and ask her how she feels about the situation at home. Give her a chance to put her picture into words. I think that venting, if you will, would be a good cleansing for her. As human beings, we all tend to keep things bottled up inside of us sometimes. This will give Jalisa a chance to let that tension go."

Mr. Sanchez and I talked for a few more minutes in which I vented a little about Tina and the problems she'd caused. He offered his opinion and gave me some advice that I appreciated. When I left his office, I left with the picture in my hand. I wanted to call Randy and tell him what had happened, but I knew it would have to wait. When Jalisa came home from school, I didn't hesitate to talk to her about her drawing.

"Jalisa, can I talk to you for a second, please?"

"But Monique, Pokémon is coming on."

"Pokémon will have to wait."

Jalisa reluctantly came into the kitchen and sat at the table. I sat down in front of her and handed her the picture she'd drawn.

"Can you tell me why you drew this, honey?"

Jalisa stared down at her artwork, but didn't speak for a long second. I could tell that she was struggling inside. I touched her cheek. "You can tell me, sweetie," I said softly. Suddenly, out of nowhere, tears began to fall from her eyes. I took her hands in mine. "Jalisa, what's wrong? Why are you crying?"

She sniffled and tried to wipe her tears away, but they kept falling. My heart ached for her. I brushed some of her tears away and kissed her forehead. "I'm here for you, angel." I didn't want to push her into talking to me, but I wanted her to know that she could confide in me.

She sniffled a few times and pouted her bottom lip. "I'm mad at Mommy," she finally said.

"Why are you mad, baby?"

"Because she's going to break you and Daddy up again."

"What makes you say that?"

"Because she did it before."

"Oh baby, your father and I had some things to work out."

"It was Mommy's fault and I know it! She's always saying nasty things to me about you, and she's always mean to you when she sees you, and then when she leaves, you and Daddy always argue. You left last time and you're going to leave again." More tears fell from her tiny eyes, causing my own tears to fall. I grabbed a napkin and dabbed hers away.

"Baby, I'm not going to leave. I'm not going anywhere. I promise."

"You did last time."

"I was just really mad at your mother and father. I had to leave to go and do some thinking. I promise I'm here to stay, okay? I'm not leaving."

"But Mommy will make you mad again."

"You're right, honey. Your mother will probably make me mad again, but you know what?"

Jalisa sniffled and rubbed her eyes. "What?"

"No matter how mad she makes me, I promise, I won't leave."

"You won't?"

"Nope."

"Promise?"

"I promise."

"I love you, Monique and I hate my mommy. I never want to see her again, and I don't want her to come and get me anymore."

I took her in my arms. "Baby, don't hate your mother, okay?" I said kissing her forehead.

"But why? She's never nice to you. And Daddy is always in a bad mood when she comes over."

"Sweetheart, your mother has problems of her own that she has to deal with. Sometimes her problems rub off on other people. Don't hate her, okay? She loves you."

"Not like you do. You don't yell at me all the time or make me do things I don't want to do."

"Sweetheart, your mother does love you. She just shows it a little differently than I do. Don't hate her. You can be mad at her sometimes, but don't hate her. She makes mistakes like we all do."

"You don't."

"Yes I do. Remember when I hit your mother in front of you? Well, that was a mistake and I was wrong for doing that. And moving out to do some thinking was a mistake too."

"It was?"

"Yes. It was."

"Did I make a mistake with my picture?"

"No, baby. Your picture was just fine." I kissed her on her forehead again and then let go of her. I slid my finger under her chin and lifted her head to look at me. "No more tears, okay?"

She nodded.

"I'm not leaving, and I don't want you to hate your mother. You tell her that you love her."

"Like I tell you?"

I smiled. "Just like you tell me." I hugged her again and smiled as she squeezed her little arms around my neck. "Now, you can still catch ten minutes of Pokémon if you hurry."

Jalisa smiled and ran out of the kitchen, leaving her picture on the table. I picked it up and looked at it again. Mr. Sanchez was right. I could see the change in Jalisa's eyes immediately. She needed to get her anger and fear out of her. I ripped up the picture in half and threw it in the garbage. I wasn't going anywhere again, no matter how much the devil tried to intervene.

That night, I spoke to Randy and told him what happened with Jalisa, and that everything had been resolved. We spoke for a few more minutes, discussing briefly his trip to the morgue, then we spoke about his visit to go and see Brian's wife the next day. I blew him a kiss and wished him a safe trip back. Before he hung up, he told me that he loved me, and I felt it deep in my soul.

Jalisa slept with me that night because she missed her daddy. I didn't mind the company either. I said a silent prayer for Travis and Randy, and then closed my eyes and hoped to recapture the dream I'd started to have earlier that day.

Randy

A group of flowers, candles, and makeshift crosses were the first things that I noticed when I approached the home where Travis was killed. I looked down briefly at the temporary memorial. Each condolence written had been for Brian and his family. Travis's name was nowhere to be found. I shook my head and continued on to the front door. I had no idea what I was going to say to Brian's widow. Hell, I didn't even know if she'd give me the opportunity to say anything at all once I'd told her who I was.

I pressed the doorbell and waited while my heart beat heavily. As I did, I wondered what had been going through my brother's mind as he had waited. When the door opened, I was greeted by a gray-haired woman, who looked to be in her late sixties or early seventies. "Can I help you?" she asked softly.

I cleared my throat. "Um, hello. I'm looking for Natalie Wilson."

The woman frowned. "Natalie's not up to seeing anyone right now."

I cleared my throat again. "Um, Mrs . . ."

"Starks."

"Mrs. Starks, my name is Randy Lincoln." I extended my hand.

"Hello, Mr. Lincoln," Mrs. Starks said, taking my hand in hers. "Are you a friend of my daughter's?"

"No, I'm not."

"Oh, then you must have been one of Brian's friends."

I cleared the nervousness from my throat once more. "No, I wasn't." I cracked my knuckle. "Mrs. Starks . . . Travis was my younger brother."

Mrs. Starks's mouth hung slightly open as she stared at me through slowly slitting eyes.

"I'd like to speak to Natalie," I said.

Mrs. Starks watched me without words for a few more seconds and then backed away and closed the door on me. I dropped my chin to my chest and exhaled, and started to regret the promise I'd made to my mother. A few seconds later, the door opened. A younger version of Mrs. Starks stood on the inside. "Please come in."

I hesitated and looked at Natalie. She had oval eyes that were red and swollen with grief. A frown seemed to encompass her entire body. I stepped inside and waited for her to close the door. Then I followed her to the living room.

"Please sit down," she said softly. I could tell by the trembling in her voice that she was desperately trying to hold back tears. I sat down across from her.

"Would you like anything to drink?"

I shook my head. "No, thank you."

Silence fell over the room for a few seconds. I really didn't know how to begin, and as I watched Natalie struggle to hold herself together, I wondered if my going there had been wise. The last thing I wanted to do was add to her pain.

"Why are you here, Mr. Lincoln?" Natalie asked me evenly.

"Call me Randy, please."

Natalie nodded and then with her eyes locked on me, asked again, "Why are you here, Randy?"

"I wanted to come and pay my respects for all that's happened."

"Did you know my husband?"

"No, I didn't."

"Did you know that your brother was seeing a married man?"

"No. I just knew that Travis was seeing someone named Paul."

A smile appeared on Natalie's face; it was obviously not a smile of pleasure.

"I guess he used his middle name for his secret life."

"I'm sorry," I said quietly.

"Sorry for what, Randy? Are you sorry for my husband marrying me and having two boys to cover up the fact that he was a homosexual? Or are you sorry that he has probably given me the HIV virus? That he's destroyed my entire world." Natalie broke down and buried her face in her hands. I sat silent and let her have her moment. "I'm sorry," she said a few minutes later, wiping her tears away with her palms. "I don't mean to be thoughtless. You lost your brother."

"It's okay," I replied. "I know this isn't easy for you."

"It can't be for you either."

I sighed. "No, it's not. But I guess given the lifestyle he'd lived and past events with your husband, I wasn't completely surprised that this happened."

Natalie looked up at me. "What do you mean by past events?"

"Travis's relationship with Brian had been volatile at times."

A fresh flow of tears fell from Natalie's eyes as she said, "How could I have not seen anything? There had to be signs. Something, anything."

She covered her face with her hands again, but this time, instead of watching, I stood up, went and sat beside her on the couch and put my arms around her. I held her tightly as she burrowed her head into my shoulder and let the river flow freely.

For ten minutes she cried and for ten minutes I patted her back softly and lent her my shoulder. I was hurting over Travis's death, but I knew that whatever I was feeling was nothing in comparison to her pain. Her husband, her best friend, her lover, her other half—gone with the possibility of leaving her HIV positive. I clenched my jaws. Life was cruel sometimes.

"I'm sorry," Natalie said, lifting her head. "I don't even know you."

I let her go. "You have nothing to apologize for."

"I wanted to hate your brother. I wanted to blame him for everything that's happened. For my world falling apart. But the more I tried, the more

I realized that the only person I could blame was Brian."

A teardrop fell from her eye as she paused and took a deep breath and exhaled slowly. I looked over at a grouping of photographs hanging on the wall above her fireplace. There were several photos of the entire family, and some of Brian and his sons. They were a perfect combination of Brian and Natalie, with her soft oval eyes and dark caramel complexion and Brian's full lips and square jaw.

"How are your sons handling all of this?"

Tears fell harder as Natalie shook her head. "They don't know yet."

"They don't?"

"No. They're away for the weekend."

"When do they come home?"

"Tonight. How am I supposed to tell them that their father, their idol, killed himself? How do I tell them that he was gay and that I may have HIV?" As Natalie covered her face and cried in agony, I sat stoic. I didn't know how to answer any of her questions. I couldn't think of anything to say that would somehow soften her blow. "I think you should go now," Natalie said, her head down, her tone defeated.

Again I tried to think of something to say. I didn't want to leave her there like that.

"Natalie—" I started.

"Please go," she said, cutting me off.

I took a deep breath and exhaled slowly and then stood up, slipped my coat on and walked away, while Natalie cried softly.

When I stepped outside, Mrs. Starks was there waiting for me. She watched me without blinking while I pulled the front door shut behind me. Her gaze actually made me nervous. I couldn't tell what she was thinking.

"I'm very sorry for everything that's happened," I said solemnly.

Mrs. Starks eyed me but didn't respond. I cleared my throat and took a step to leave.

"I always had a feeling that he was gay," Mrs. Starks said suddenly.

I turned and faced her.

"There was just always something about him that seemed funny. Something about the way he moved, talked, and treated my daughter. I looked at their pictures today and I could see his homosexuality plain as day. I could see it in the way he held Natalie. There was a slight distance that he always seemed to keep. You can see it in each picture. If you look really close, you could almost see that his smile hadn't been a smile at all, but a widened frown."

She paused to take a breath and then looked up toward the darkening sky. I stood motionless and silent.

"I wanted to say something to her a long time ago when they first started getting serious. I wanted to lift the veil from her eyes. Help her see what I saw. But then she got pregnant, and he proposed and I kept my mouth shut. Now my daughter may be HIV positive. You have nothing to be sorry for, Mr. Lincoln. If anyone is to be sorry, it's me. I should have opened my mouth. I should have said something."

Mrs. Starks touched me lightly on my arm and then walked inside, leaving me alone. I shook my head and then walked away. I paused by the memorial and said a prayer, not only for Travis, but for Mrs. Starks, Natalie, and her boys.

I told my mother and Monique about my visit when I got back to New York, and I shared with them Mrs. Starks' admission. They both cried and said silent prayers. I held onto Jalisa tightly after telling her what happened to her Uncle Travis. She didn't know him well, but she knew him enough to shed tears. As expected, my father didn't share our sentiment.

Travis's funeral service was supposed to have been a private affair. I'd really only wanted the immediate family to be there, which meant me, Monique, Jalisa, and my mother. But the news about his death circled around throughout the gay community, and before I knew it, the small affair turned out to be one with over two hundred people. They were Travis's friends, former lovers, and people he'd never even known. All had come to pay their respects to one who had fallen. Several of them made speeches during the service. One person's speech in particular moved me and touched my soul. The speech that was given was by Travis's best friend from the past, Vanessa. She'd found out about his death and had come back to pay her respects to a friend she'd let go.

She talked about old times with Travis and about the things they used to do. She spoke about his wishes when he was younger, and how he wanted to be a fashion designer when he grew older. She brought a smile to everyone's face as she mentioned how they pretended to be a couple in order to keep his homosexuality a secret. I learned things about my brother that I never knew. I also learned how devastating it had been for him to lose the love from Abe and our father. I never realized how lonely he felt, or that he'd considered suicide at times, in the hopes that everyone else's lives could go back to being normal. Vanessa's words were moving, uplifting, and sad at the same time. The most moving part of her eulogy, however, was when she talked about her own decision to abandon Travis.

"I chose a man over my best friend who would have given his life to save me. I gave up a friendship that was blessed by the hand of God, all for a man who disrespected me and disrespected our union. Travis was my heart and I will always regret that I wasn't there for him when he needed me the most. Travis, I never forgot about you," she'd said, looking at his open casket. "Not a day went by where you weren't in my thoughts, in my prayers, and in my heart. You touched me deeper than any man I've ever loved could have. You made me feel like a beautiful, strong woman, who could do anything and be anyone I desired to be. I love you, Travis, and I beg for your forgiveness."

Vanessa shed violent tears at the podium, as she was unable to hold back her grief. She cried for a few minutes without interruption and then walked out of the church.

My mother too, was unable to contain herself, as she fell to the ground in a fit of tears. No one

touched her as she cried. She'd earned that soli-
tary moment. I cried too. I cried for the pain
Travis had lived, the abandonment he'd endured,
and the life he'd had taken away.

After the service, we went to a reception hall for
a going-home celebration. I'd never been around
that many homosexuals before, and as I shook
hands with them and exchanged hugs as they offered their condolences, I took solace in knowing
that my brother hadn't been as alone as I thought
he might have been. Theirs was a strong community, filled with love and understanding; a brother-
hood and sisterhood that many of us heterosexuals
would never fully comprehend or experience. My
mother walked around mingling and smiling.
When I asked her how she'd overcome her grief,
she explained to me that her tears during the service had not been tears of pain.

"Those were tears of joy," she'd said. "Travis was
finally set free and has gone on to a better place
where he doesn't have to worry about being
ridiculed, criticized, patronized, hated or scorned."

I had to agree.

Abe's wife Nakyia was also at the funeral. She
wanted to pay her respects for a brother-in-law
she'd never met. Abe, of course, didn't come. I
found out from Nakyia that Brian had been Abe's
director at work. I can't lie: I wanted to laugh.
Okay, maybe I did just a little. How could I not?
The irony was amazing. All the time and energy
Abe had wasted on his homophobia and here it
was that his boss was living in the closet and sleeping with Travis. How cruel and funny was that?
Nakyia filled me in on how messed up Abe was

over the revelation. Again, I couldn't help but laugh a little. Abe was now forever tied to Travis in more ways than he'd ever wanted to be.

As far as I was concerned, he deserved what he got.

I hugged Nakyia and wished her well before she left. She smiled and told me that there would be major changes with her life in the near future. Although she hadn't given me any more information, I had a feeling about what some of those major changes were going to be. I gave her a kiss on her cheek and told her not to be a stranger. With a good-bye she walked away.

Monique talked with a few of Travis's friends and smiled at me whenever I looked over at her. I had an engagement ring for her. Tina had called and cursed me out for having Monique as the second point of contact at school and her as the third. I hung up on her before she had a chance to say anything else. I did mention to her that I would be marrying Monique before I did, though.

Jalisa sat with my mother and entertained everyone. She'd held up well despite knowing that her uncle was gone, but that was because he'd never come around much, so she'd never really gotten a chance to get close to him.

As people sat and ate cake and sipped on punch, I stepped outside to get some fresh, crisp night air. I was looking up at the dark sky, contemplating life without Travis when a voice that I never expected to hear again called out my name.

"Hello, Randy."

I turned around. "Natalie?" Natalie walked up to

me slowly and gave me a half smile. "What are you doing here?"

"Some of Brian's other *associates* came by the house to pay their respects. They also knew your brother. Or at least knew of him. They told me about the funeral. I wanted to pay my respects."

I took her hand. "Thank you for coming. I know this isn't easy for you."

Natalie shrugged her shoulders. "It couldn't have been easy for you when you came."

I nodded my head. "So how are you holding up?"

Natalie sighed and for a moment it seemed as though she was going to cry. But she didn't.

"Well, it's official—I am HIV positive. I got the results a few days ago."

I clenched my jaws. "I'm sorry," I said softly.

"To answer your question, I'm managing the best I can under the circumstances that I was forced into. I'd like to say that with time things will get better, but unfortunately for me they won't."

"Don't lose hope," I said, trying to lift her spirits.

"It's not that I've lost hope. I've just accepted the reality of my situation. I don't have Magic Johnson money. I can't afford the special medications to fight the disease like he can. All I can do is take what all of the normal people are taking. Sometimes I break down and cry when I think about everything. I was married to Brian for nineteen years and I never had a clue. I should have seen something, shouldn't I?"

"Don't put that burden on your shoulders,

Natalie. Brian hid his secret from everyone." Natalie didn't reply. A few seconds of silence passed before I asked, "How are your sons dealing with everything?"

Natalie sighed again, and this time tears fell slowly. "They are having a rough time. My oldest, Dominic, especially. He's your typical teenage jock: all sports, and only cheerleaders. He's very homophobic, and finding out that his father was gay is really tearing him apart emotionally. He's quit the basketball team because he doesn't want to deal with the stares and questions, and comments going on behind his back. I'm really worried about him. I don't want his life to be destroyed because of his father's secret. I try to talk to him about it, but he rejects my efforts and just shuts me and everyone else out."

"What are his feelings about Brian's suicide?"

"Honestly, I think his father being gay is affecting him much more than the suicide. He hasn't said anything, but I have a feeling that he feels relief that he won't have to deal with his father."

"Have you tried to take him to a psychiatrist? Maybe it would be easier for him to talk to a stranger."

Natalie nodded. "I finally convinced him to see a doctor next week. I'm praying that the doctor will be able to get him to open up and bring out the anger that he's bottling up inside."

"What about your youngest? How is he?"

"Brandon is handling things a little better. He's just as angry and feels just as betrayed, but his mind isn't as narrow. He doesn't seem to have the same type of homophobia that Dominic has. I think he's going to be okay in the long run. We'll see, I guess. All I can do is be there for support and hope for the best."

"That really is all you can do. Ultimately, they'll both have to make their own decisions about how they want to deal with everything."

"I know."

"How did they take the news about the HIV?"

Natalie folded her arms across her chest. "I haven't told them yet."

"You haven't?"

"No. This whole situation has been so traumatic for them that I just don't know how to break the news to them. I know that it's better for them to deal with everything all at once, but how do I do it? How do I tell my babies that I'm going to die?"

"Try not to think that way, Natalie. You don't know what may happen in the future. Remember—you have the virus, but you don't have AIDS."

"I know. And I know that it may never become full-blown. But believe me, from where I'm standing having HIV is like being given a death sentence. I just don't know the date of my execution yet."

"None of us know."

Natalie gave another half smile. "No. I guess not. Anyway, enough about me and my misery—how are you holding up?"

"I'm hanging in there. It's a little hard knowing that he's gone and never coming back, but I know that he's in a better place."

"And your family?"

"Well, my mom's handling it well. Better than I

thought she would, actually. As far as my brother and father go—remember when we were talking about your sons having to make their own decisions?"

"Yeah."

"Well, my father gave up on Travis a long time ago, so he's not here, and my brother, who gave up on Travis also, is at home battling with his own demons."

"What do you mean?"

"My brother worked with Brian, Natalie."

"What?"

"My brother's name is Abraham, but he goes by Abe."

"Oh, my God! Abe is your brother? He's been to the house before. He and Brian used to golf frequently. He's not gay too is he?"

I shook my head.

"Are you two close?"

"We used to be," I said evenly. I didn't say anything more.

Noticing my reluctance to speak on that further, Natalie took my hand and smiled. "I'm glad I came."

"I am too."

Natalie looked toward the hall's entrance where a few people were standing outside smoking cigarettes. "I take it Travis had a lot of friends?"

"Yeah. I had no idea he had this many. If there's one thing I can say about the gay community I've learned thus far, it's that they really do support one another. I think Travis is resting easier knowing that his friends would be there for him."

"I'm glad for him. You know, I found out something interesting about Brian."

"What's that?"

"My mother-in-law told me that when he was
thirteen, she found him masturbating to gay
porno magazines."

"Really?"

"Really. She said she beat him until he bled and
that after that she never had a problem with him
doing that again. She thought he was going
through a phase then. I guess no one realized his
phase took him all the way through adulthood. It's
funny . . . I want to hate him so bad for everything,
but I just can't, because he took care of his family.
I can never say that he wasn't there when he was
needed. Family was truly number one for him, and
because of that, I'll always love him." Natalie
paused and took a breath. "Randy, I want to apologize for the pain Brian has caused all of you. I wish
I could bring your brother back. I wish I could
erase everything he did."

"No apologies necessary, Natalie. My family is
going to be fine. Nothing has really changed for
us, although Abe's now been forced to accept the
fact that being gay doesn't mean you're any less of
a person. I think he had this stereotype about
them and their lifestyle. I think he only saw nega-
tivity. And you know, at times I did too." I put out
my hand. "If anything, I hope I can say that I've
gotten a new friend."

Natalie smiled. "Definitely," she said, giving me
a hug.

We held onto one another for a few seconds

more, and when we let go, Natalie smiled. "I'm going to go inside."

"I'll be in soon. I need to do something first."

Natalie walked off, leaving me alone. I looked up to the black sky again and said my own private good-bye to my brother. It was now his turn to watch out for me.

Nakyia

The day I told Abe good-bye had been the final part of my three-step process of letting my old life go. I'd come up with this three-step plan the night I followed him and verified that he was cheating on me. We were at the beach, taking advantage of one of my good days, when I'd made the decision to play detective. Abe thought I had been asleep and hadn't noticed his cell phone vibrating, but I wasn't. My eyes were closed and I was enjoying the sounds of the beach's activity; the waves breaking and crashing on the sand, children screaming happily, seagulls talking to each other in the sky above. I was at peace, enjoying it all until that call came. I had my eyes open just a fraction when he grabbed his cell and checked the caller ID. At first I was going to give him the benefit of the doubt and believe that it was a call he didn't want. But when he took the phone with him on his "stroll" on the beach, I knew right then and there that my fear and suspicions about my husband were valid.

When he came back and told me that he had to go in to work, I struggled to mask my hurt. My nerve was hurting, but it wasn't as bad as I let on, and when Abe left for the office, I waited a few minutes before I hopped in my car. I cried as I drove down Highway 95. I'd been trying to deny what I knew was the truth for so long. All of the signs had been there: late and extra weekend hours, showers after those hours, disinterest in sex. I was never blind to any of it. I just chose to deal with it because I knew that my affliction had been a strain on both of us.

I went searching for the truth that particular night because the day at the beach was supposed to be my day. I wanted to enjoy it, pain or no pain. To know that he couldn't give me that was the ultimate offense. That was the last time I would allow him to disappoint me.

I stayed hidden where I couldn't be seen and watched Abe go into the building alone. A few minutes later, the very person he was supposed to be going into work for, Taki, pulled into the lot. It was humid as hell and there was no rain, yet she'd been wearing a trench coat. I didn't need to see anymore. I left after that and devised my plan.

Step one was for me to have my surgery.

I wanted my life to change and the only way for that to happen was to get rid of the one thing that had truly been a roadblock to happiness and a normal life. I wanted to stop taking the medication day in and day out. I was fed up with the drugged-out feeling that had become the norm for me. I wanted to eat, talk, smile, and laugh without a care in the world. I went home that night and weighed the pros and cons and then decided that the risks were worth it.

Step two took place before and after the surgery.

I had to truly come to grips with Abe's infidelity. Even though I'd accepted the truth, I still had to search within myself to know that his cheating had not been my fault. Initially I started to beat myself up emotionally with negative thoughts, thinking that had I never gotten the neuralgia, Abe would have never cheated. Had I been able to do all of the things any other woman could do, he would have never strayed.

But as my spirit and self-esteem became stronger I realized that I was wrong on those and many other accounts. I came to understand that Abe's unfaithfulness had more to do with him being a weak man, than it did my being sick. I wasn't to blame and I'd be damned if I, or anyone else, tried to make me feel that way. Now that I'd had the surgery and had seen Abe for what he was—a pathetic excuse for a man, the time had come to move on to step number three.

I had to say good-bye to Abe and walk away from my marriage.

"Abe, I'm leaving."

Abe looked at me with confusion in his eyes. "Leaving? What do you mean?"

"I know all about you and Taki," I said evenly. I was determined to stay calm and not let my anger get the best of me. I wanted to stay above the ignorance I could have unleashed.

"Me and Taki? What are you talking about?"

I put up my hand.

"Before you go any further, let me just say that I went to Taki's home to confront the bitch, but she wasn't there, so I ended up having a nice, long conversation with her husband, who was actually there packing his things. I'm sure you know by now that he's leaving her." Abe opened his mouth to respond but I wouldn't let him. "I've had it with your disrespect for me and the vows we made. When I woke up after the surgery and I didn't feel pain, I felt like almost all of the weight had been lifted from my shoulders. Almost. But there was just one more thing weighing me down that I needed to get rid of. You know what, Abe? That one thing was you. Pain or no pain, I deserved a man who would have stood strong by my side and never strayed. The vows say through sickness and health. When my sickness came you deserted me, just like you did Travis."

I paused to catch my breath. It felt great to release my pain and anger.

"Nakyia . . . let me explain . . ."

"I don't want any explanations, Abe."

"Baby, please . . . believe me, it's over between her and me. I want to be with you, Nakyia. Don't leave me now. I need you. Travis's death—"

"Means absolutely nothing to you. Don't you dare expect me to feel pity for you."

"But Nakyia . . . you're better. You can do—"

"I can do what?" I asked, cutting him off. "I can suck your dick without it hurting me?"

"Come on, Nakyia. Be fair to me."

"Be fair?"

"Yes! Damn it, you weren't the only one hurting,

you know. I may not have been in pain but I lost something too. I lost a partner. Everything changed after the neuralgia! You, me, us—nothing was the same anymore."

"Abe, you were the only one who changed. I was in pain, but through it all I remained the same person."

"Oh, come on," Abe screamed. "You were not the same person and you know it! You became a distant, unaffectionate, depressing person. It wasn't easy being around you. It wasn't easy being with someone that you couldn't kiss, couldn't talk to, and couldn't smile with. You were not the Nakyia I married!"

"How can you be so damn unfair and selfish? Do you think I asked for the neuralgia? Do you think I wanted it? I was in pain every waking day. Do you think I didn't want to smile? Do you think that I didn't want to do every normal thing that I used to do? How dare you accuse me of changing! How dare you throw that in my face! Abe, you could have been on your deathbed and I would have never, never left your side!"

"Nakyia—"

"Nakyia, nothing!" I screamed, as tears streamed down my cheeks. I'd reached my emotional breaking point and I could no longer fight back the turmoil I was feeling inside. "Go and be with Taki! You two are now free to fuck each other all you want!"

I grabbed my bag and when he tried to prevent me from leaving, I kneed him in his balls. He's lucky that's all I did.

Although it was tough in the beginning, I learned that I could be on my own and love life more than I'd ever loved it. Abe and his companionship were gone but I had my pride and dignity intact. Abe lost out. With my nerve problem gone, some lucky man was going to get the best of me.

Abe

Nothing had been the same for me since Travis died. It was kind of funny, actually. As much as I wanted to have nothing to do with him, I'm now tied to him more than anyone else in my life. For years I refused to acknowledge him as my brother. I didn't want to be associated with him. I didn't want to be exposed to his lifestyle. I guess I was just afraid, though I don't really know why. Travis was my brother. Plain and simple. Gay or straight, nothing would ever change that.

So why did I abandon my own flesh and blood?

I could think of a few words: naive, ignorant, immature, cruel, cold, and selfish. I could probably keep going. Or maybe I could use one word to summarize everything.

Stupid.

That's all it was.

Stupid.

All of the other words line up underneath it, like *A*, *B*, and *C* points in an outline. I let my own stupidity destroy my relationship with Travis. I couldn't help but laugh sometimes. While I lived my life supposedly untouched by his homosexuality, I was slapping myself in the face with it day in and day out. When God wants to let you know that you've been wrong, He sure does it right.

It took me a good six months to get past the fact that Brian had been gay and that I'd been as close to him as I was. In the beginning, after I found out the truth, I threw up anytime I would think about how we'd gone on the business trip and he called me for a condom.

My own brother.

What were the chances of something like that happening?

I never thought my life would end up the way it had. Randy and I had started to speak again, but we were nowhere as close to being as tight as we used to be. I try to reach out to him, but he won't open up with me. He's still pissed about my reaction to Travis's death, and that I never bothered to show up at the funeral service. Now that I'd had time to sit and think, I can't say that I blame him. But at the time I just couldn't go. I wasn't ready to face anything. I wasn't ready to look down on my brother's grave. The whole situation was just too real for me. The day I found out Brian was Travis's lover and murderer, replayed in my mind over and over like a scratch on a CD. I could only hope that the painful memory faded away in time. I hope that in time my relationship with Randy heals. Of course, I knew that the responsibility primarily fell on my shoulders. I guess it was time I own up to a lot of things.

I had to do that after Nakyia left me. When she

confronted me about Taki, I was shocked. All this time I thought I had the wool pulled over her eyes and the whole time she'd been the one fooling me. When she left, she bruised not only my balls, but my pride too. She was right. I was the only one who changed in our relationship. I became selfish. I ignored her needs and pushed to the darkest corners of my mind, just what she'd been going through.

I was so alone after she left. I tried to call her and beg her to come back. I needed her in so many ways. Her companionship, her love, her support. I wanted to tell her all of that, but she never returned any of my calls. Without her, my healing process was so much harder.

After Brian's suicide, Taki was given his position at work. I quit before she could fire me. I'd been humiliated enough and the last thing I was going to do was give her the satisfaction of using her authority to smile in my face and take my job away again. I never did see or hear from her after I turned in my resignation. I did hear through some mutual business partners that she'd lost her parental right to her girls because it was discovered that she had an addiction to cocaine that no one had known about. That secret was blown when a friend of Whilice's saw her at a party snorting in the guest bathroom.

I bumped into Whilice once at the gym. We didn't exchange any words as we stared at one another, but I did have my fists ready just in case he wanted to come at me. I know in his position I would have come at me. But he never did. He simply frowned and then walked away. Although he may never admit it, I think he was secretly relieved to be rid of Taki.

Once I left the job, I went into a hibernation of sorts. I didn't go anywhere, didn't do anything, and I didn't call anyone. I kept to myself and my solitude. I did take time to sign the divorce papers that Nakyia had sent to me. But I didn't do that until I made one last effort to get her back. I called her, hoping that maybe I would be able to convince her that I'd realized the error of my ways and that the man she knew and fell in love with was back and ready to love and treat her like a queen again.

Our phone conversation had been cordial, short, and hurtful. Nakyia had no desire to come back to me. There was a joy and peace in her tone that I hadn't heard in a long time. I could practically see her smiling into the receiver when we talked, and I knew that had nothing to do with me. Or maybe it did. Maybe my fooling around had been what she'd needed.

Another slap in the face for me.

I never tried to call her again after that, and that night I signed the papers and sent them on the next day.

Losing Randy's respect and Nakyia's heart left me lonely. For the first time that I could ever remember, no one was there for me. My mother was there of course, but the same disappointment resonated in her voice as it had in Randy's.

I don't remember when I'd made the decision to go to Travis's grave. I guess it must have been somewhere in between my feelings of regret and sadness. All I know is that I got in my car one rainy morning, turned the key in the ignition, and drove.

And now there I was, looking down on a brother I'd deserted years ago. A brother who I knew deep in my soul, had the roles been reversed, would have never done as I had. I didn't speak for a few minutes. I just stood silent while the heavy rain beat down on me, soaking me from head to toe. I didn't care that thunder was exploding in the sky or that lighting streaked above me; I was oblivious to it all. There was nothing but myself and my brother's final resting place.

How could I have disrespected him the way I had?

How could I have never attended the going-home service?

I wanted to cry as I asked myself those and other questions, but I didn't, because I didn't feel I had the right to. I took a look up towards the sky and exhaled away all of the stress that had been weighing me down. With one final crackle in the gray sky, I went down to my knees, touched my brother's headstone, and said the first and only thing that came to my mind.

"Travis . . . I'm sorry."

SIX MONTHS LATER

Taki

"What do you mean there's someone else?" I stood in shock before my new man as he sat at the breakfast table facing me as though his statement hadn't been a big deal. I met A'sahn at a time when my life had completely bottomed out.

After Whilice left me, I thought my life was going to get better. I'd finally managed to get rid of his lead-weighted ass and I'd finally gotten the position that I'd paid my dues for in more ways than one. It was still hard to believe that Brian was gay and had killed himself and his lover. Working in advertising I've come across many, many men who were either out of the closet or standing in there with the door cracked enough to let me know that they liked to play both sides of the field. But Brian had been damn good at keeping his door closed with a padlock, and all of the slits blocked to prevent any peeking. Now I understood why he never tried to sleep with me, which is what all of my other bosses had done; this included Brian's geriatric-looking director. All this time I'd been assuming that Brian was one of the last few faithful men in this world, when he was actually getting his groove on with Abe's brother. I found that out from a gay friend of mine at the gym. I'd tried to call Abe after I found out, but he never answered any of my calls.

After Brian's suicide and Abe's resignation, I felt like a queen on the throne. I thought I was untouchable. Whilice moved out, Brian was no longer in my way, and I didn't have to worry about my affair with Abe coming out at work. Everything seemed to be going the way it always should have.

But then my secret was revealed.

I'd been using cocaine for a little over two years. I'd started after a business meeting with a client that I didn't want to lose. I invited him out for drinks after our all-day meeting, to celebrate what I hoped would be his signing on the dotted line. I took the contract with me. While we sat at our table, I tried to discuss my business plan further and forecast for his company. Well into our third glass of champagne, it was obvious that the last thing he wanted to do was talk shop. I'd been through the drill before, so I endured his flirting and touching of my thigh, and then went with him to his hotel. That wasn't the first time I'd slept with a client for their John Hancock, so it was no big deal to me. I figured it would be as easy as one, two, three. I'd go in, ride him for a couple of minutes, lying about how good he felt and how he was making me feel until he came, and then leave him with a smile and my contract signed. If there was any one thing I'd learned from my years as an

ambitious and determined woman in the male-
dominated world of business, it was that you had
to do whatever was necessary to climb up the lad-
der. It was all very routine, really.

Unfortunately, someone forgot to send me the
memo telling me that the routine had been
changed.

We went up into his room, and as I started to
slide out of my dress, the client pulled out a silver
tray with several lines of coke on it. I'd never tried
drugs before that, and I wasn't about to start then.
I told him no and said that the sex would make up
for it, but he wasn't trying to hear that.

"A high fuck is the best kind," he'd said.

I told him no again, but then he threatened to
take his business over to another advertising firm;
namely our competitor. I hadn't yet become head
of the East Coast division of the company and I
knew that my capturing that position was dependent on the client signing the contract.

Because of my ambitions, I gave in and snorted
two lines.

I don't actually remember much about the sex
we had, although both of my holes hurt for the
next few days. The only thing I remember was the
feeling of absolute euphoria I had. For years I'd
been searching for that ultimate high, only I'd
been doing it through my accomplishments at
work. But no matter how many hours I'd put in or
what I'd achieved, I'd never found it. I'd never
truly been satisfied until that cocaine ran wild
through my bloodstream. I wasn't riding my client
that night. I was riding a cloud, soaring high in the

clear blue sky with rays of sunlight washing over me while the harmonious sounds of harps sighed in the breeze.

I'd been searching for that first-time high ever since. And I was searching for it the night Whilice's coworker walked in on me in the bathroom of my girlfriend's house. I didn't know that he was dating my girlfriend's sister. He didn't hesitate to run and tell Whilice what he saw, not even after I gave him a blow job.

With my secret revealed and my affair with Abe exposed, the judge ordered me to rehab and gave full custody of my daughters to their father, who only hated me more after that. Losing my girls devastated me. So did the look of shame, disappointment, and anger written on my oldest daughter's face. With the girls gone and my reputation at work damaged because of my drug habit, I spiraled into a state of depression and stayed there until A'sahn came along.

We met at the club. I was out trying to have a good time when he approached me and without asking, grabbed my hand and took me out to the dance floor.

"You didn't think to ask?" I said with my ass against his crotch.

"You didn't think to say no?" he said, thrusting into me.

It was an immediate attraction. We exchanged numbers that night, and started seeing each other soon after that. A'sahn was the bad boy with style that I'd always wanted. Even though he's younger than I am, he had his shit together. At twenty-eight, he's very successful. He owns two of the hottest hip-hop clubs in Miami. That was one of his clubs that we were in. A'sahn is a lighter version of Mekhi Phifer, only with no hair. He's tall, lean, and knows how to wear the hell out of designer clothing. Best of all, having sex with A'sahn was like having sex with Abe only multiplied by three. A'sahn always left me breathless after our bouts of lovemaking, and unlike Whilice, who liked to get in and get out before I had a chance to blink, he took the time to admire and savor every one of my curves. He touched me in places and ways that I didn't even touch myself, and after being with Whilice's unsatisfying ass, I'd gotten to know my body pretty damn well.

After Whilice, and after Abe, I never planned on falling in love again. But the more time that passed with A'sahn, the more I found myself doing just that. He helped bring me out of a pit I didn't think I was going to rise from. With him I could hold my head up high and not give a shit about the people who looked down on me with scorn.

"What do you mean there's someone else?" I asked again. I was still in my bathrobe, naked underneath. A'sahn looked at me and then looked away.

"I mean I'm not feeling you anymore, Taki. I mean you fine and all, but you just not doin' it for me anymore."

I put my hand on my hips. "Not doing it for you anymore? What the fuck kind of bullshit is that? That's not what you said to me last night!"

A'sahn laughed. "Shorty, I was bustin' a nut."

"You son of a bitch!" I reached out and tried to slap him, but he caught me by my wrist.

"Don't even think about it, Taki. You know I don't play." He pushed me back and stood up.

I struggled to keep my composure and keep tears back. "But A'sahn, I thought we had something. I love you, and I thought you loved me too."

A'sahn chuckled again as he slid his cell phone into his Sean John jeans. "Love? Taki, I'm twenty-eight years old with an empire to build. I ain't tryin' to fall in love with nobody, no time soon."

"So who's this other bitch?"

A'sahn rubbed his hands together, nodded up and down repeatedly and bit down on his bottom lip. "She's my new flavor of the month."

"So that's all I ever was to you? A flavor? A fuck?"

"You said it, not me."

"Get the fuck out of my house!"

"My car's in the shop, baby doll. I need a ride."

"You say there's another woman and then you have the nerve to ask me for a ride. Get the hell out, you ignorant son of a bitch!"

A'sahn chuckled again and then said, "Well, can we at least fuck one last time?"

I screamed out again as A'sahn laughed and walked past me. I wanted to strike out and hit him, but I was afraid to. He walked out of my house and when he closed the door behind him, I threw a vase filled with flowers he'd given me and screamed out as the glass shattered into tiny pieces. I moved from the vase to the plates I'd set out for breakfast and threw them too. I let the tears leak from my eyes as I lashed out.

"Not fair!" I yelled. "It's not fair!"

I sank down to the ground in a fit of tears and wondered why A'sahn had hurt me the way he had. I'd been so good to him; treated him the way I thought he wanted to be treated. What had I done wrong?

I slowly rose from the ground and went to the window to see if A'sahn was standing outside. Despite the things he'd said, I wanted to talk to him one more time to see if I could change his mind. Maybe I would give him that fuck he'd asked for. Although after the way I planned to work it, I don't think it would have been the last. Hell, I'd make him forget all about the other flavor.

He was standing by the curb on his phone laughing. I knocked on the window, trying to get his attention. When he didn't answer, I avoided the glass and pieces of china, and stepped outside. I called A'sahn's name out loud. He didn't turn around.

"A'sahn!" I called again.

Just then a red convertible Mitsubishi Spider appeared from around the corner and came to a stop in front of him. A woman wearing shades and a baseball cap was driving the car. I tried to get a good look at her, to see what kind of flavor she was, but A'sahn was in the way. I called out his name as he opened the door to get in. This time he turned around.

"What do you want, Taki?"

As I stepped toward him to tell him what I wanted, my name was screamed out loud.

"Taki?"

Both A'sahn and I looked to the woman who was now getting out of her car.

"Taki as in you fucked my husband, Abe?"

I squinted my eyes. "Nakyia?"

Nakyia walked around her car to the curb and stood with her hands on her hips.

"You know her?" A'sahn asked, looking at her.

Eyeing me with venom, Nakyia said, "Remember when I told you about the bitch Abe was screwing? Well, she's the bitch."

A'sahn burst out laughing. "Oh shit! Are you for real?" He turned to me. "You were fucking Abe?"

"You know Abe?" I asked. "What's going on? What are you doing here, Nakyia?"

"You really are pathetic, Taki," Nakyia said, walking toward me. "A'sahn is my cousin."

"Your cousin?" I couldn't believe it. "You planned this shit, didn't you, bitch! You set this all up to get back at me for giving Abe what you couldn't. And you have the nerve to call me pathetic." I turned to A'sahn, who was standing at the side laughing. "This isn't funny, you immature ass."

"Don't talk to my cousin that way, bitch!" Nakyia snapped. "His hooking up with your ass is purely coincidental. Believe me, the last thing I would ever do is waste my time on someone as cheap and trifling as you. You are below me. I mean, look at you. You had a husband and what did you do? You slept with my husband and then moved from him to my younger, more immature cousin. No offense, A'sahn."

"None taken, 'cuz."

"Taki, you have absolutely no respect for yourself. I met your husband. I've seen pictures of your girls. I saw the life you gave up. The life you never valued. Only a foolish woman would let all of that go. I can't believe I ever lost sleep over Abe being with you. I'm so glad the world is this small because it's given me an opportunity to see just how much you and Abe deserved one another. Enjoy your life, Taki, because I damn sure will. A'sahn . . . are you staying?"

A'sahn looked at me while I stood speechless. I wanted to snap back at Nakyia for the things she'd said. I wanted to spit curse words at her. I wanted to tell her that her words meant nothing to me. That they hadn't affected me. But the truth was they had. She was right. . . . I'd given up so much.

As A'sahn smiled mockingly at me, and Nakyia turned her back and walked away, I'd never felt like more of a fool. My husband, who'd loved, respected, and adored me; my daughters, my family, my coworkers—I'd lost respect from them all, and I had no one to blame.

A'sahn approached me. "You still want to give it to me?"

"Go to hell, A'sahn!"

With nothing else to say, I turned around and walked back inside. Before I closed the door, the last thing I heard was A'sahn's mocking laughter.

Questions for Discussions

1. Abe had deep hatred/resentment for Travis. Why do you think he did?

2. Although he didn't agree with Travis's lifestyle, Randy never disowned him. Would you have done the same with your own brother, sister, son or daughter?

3. Why do you think Travis put up with Brian's abuse? Was he truly in love with him?

4. Taki had issues with her husband Whilice . . . were they warranted?

5. Did Abe get what he deserved in the end?

6. Did Tina truly want to be a "family" with Randy?

7. Was Abe wrong for cheating on Nakyia? Or was there room for justification considering her affliction?

8. Monique truly loved Randy. Did she put up with too much, for too long? Would you have given up on the relationship?

9. Do you think Abe and Randy will ever be close again?

10. What—if anything—do you think Abe learned from Travis' death?

COMING IN SEPTEMBER 2010

EYE FOR AN EYE

BY DWAYNE S. JOSEPH

Prologue

"Amado Mio."

Playing from my iPod in the living room.

"Amado Mio" by Pink Martini.

I leaned my head back. Listened to the melody. Felt my skin tingle. The breakdown was coming. My skin always tingled when it did.

"Amado Mio."

Like sex, the song was that good. That sexy. That intense. That powerful. If there were a movie about me, this would be my theme song.

I closed my eyes.

Breathed slowly.

Ran my hands up my thighs, past my stomach, over my erect nipples, to my neck, then back down again.

I was wet from the hot water covering me. I was dripping from the melodic orgasm Pink Martini and their groove had caused. Every woman needs to own a copy of this song.

It was the perfect size. The prefect width. The perfect stroke.

To hell with a dick. Just put this song on repeat. Ringing.

There was no ringing in the song.

I opened my eyes and looked over to my right. My BlackBerry was on the rim of my tub, ringing softly, the volume set at level two. I sighed. I was in mid-stroke, nearing self-fulfilled ecstasy. I should have turned the damn thing off.

I reached over and grabbed it with my fingers wet from the water and my pussy. A Friday night, nearing nine-thirty. Aida followed the rules. Only one other person who didn't.

I connected the call and placed the BlackBerry against my ear. "Marlene."

"We have a potential client."

I exhaled. "It's Friday night, Marlene."

"I know I'm not supposed to call."

"Yet you did."

"I'm sorry, but—"

"Friday nights are off limits."

Marlene sighed apologetically. I could see her running her hands through her hair. She said, "I know. I tried not to call, but she sounds desperate. She wants to know if you'll help her tonight."

In the background, "Amado Mio" had finished and was restarting. I'd heard the song thousands of times, but each time was like hearing it for the first time. I hated missing any of the song. "Give it to Aida."

"You've given the last three clients to her."

"And she's done well with them."

"It's been four months since you've taken a client on."

"And?"

"Lisette . . ." Marlene paused momentarily. I could tell she was trying to choose her words carefully. "I know I've asked you this before, but are you sure you're all right? Believe me, you are the strongest person I know, but after everything you went through with Kyra . . . I would understand if you were a bit scared."

I closed my eyes and shook my head.

That name.

Kyra.

Almost a year ago, she'd taken me to the edge. She thought she'd been on my level. Thought she'd been better than me.

She'd been wrong.

But she had taken me to the edge.

She'd caused things to happen. Things that kept me from getting a full night's sleep. Things that had me on edge. Things that had indeed scarred me. Of course, I would never admit it to anyone. Marlene had seen me at my weakest point and that would be all she would ever see.

I said, "I'm fine."

"Lisette . . . I know you don't like to admit it, but you are human."

"I'm fine," I said again.

Marlene wouldn't let up. "She had you beaten and raped. I don't know anyone who can go through that and remain unscathed."

"I said I'm fine, Marlene."

"Then why haven't you taken on any clients, Lisette?"

I clenched my jaw.

Two years ago, I became a home wrecker: a woman hired by wives to "ruin" their marriages.

They sought my services for various reasons. Some were women who'd become fed up with their husbands' infidelity. They wanted evidence to use against them to help garner the best payoff possible. Some women were victims of emotional, physical, or verbal abuse who felt trapped and saw my "expertise" as a means of escape. Other women weren't seeking an escape or a big payday. They just wanted leverage. Something to hold over their husbands' heads so that they could do whatever the hell they wanted to do. Pictures, videos, sometimes the satisfaction of walking in and seeing their cheating bastards in compromising situations—whatever they wanted, I provided.

Marlene had been my first client. A fear of scrutiny from her friends and family kept her hostage in a marriage to a pathetic asshole. I gave Marlene the same thing I gave my clients after her—the very thing that I got off on.

Control.

Marlene and all of the other clients had none. That meant they had no power. I'd learned a long time ago that life without control wasn't life at all. Life without control was death. Life without control just didn't make any sense to me. Before I helped her, Marlene was weak. She changed when she got control back.

Kyra had managed to take my control away from me. She'd managed to render me powerless. Although I'd never told her directly, Marlene's newfound strength had been what pulled me away from the edge of insanity I'd been teetering on. Before my services, Marlene had been an acquaintance. Now . . . she was a friend—my only real friend— and despite the fact that I never called her that, she knew it, and I appreciated her for that.

"For the last time . . . I'm fine," I said. "I haven't been in the mood to take on any clients."

"Lisette—"

"Give the client to Aida."

Marlene was silent for a moment before sighing and saying, "OK."

"I'm going to go back and enjoy my Friday night now."

"Are you listening to your song again?"

"Of course."

"Can I ask you something?"

I pressed down on my eyeballs with the middle finger and thumb of my free hand. I exhaled. "What?"

"That song . . . it's about love. Why do you like it so much?"

I opened my eyes and looked toward the living room. The breakdown in the song was coming again.

It was a valid question.

I didn't believe in any of the song's lyrics, yet the song resonated and stoked a fire inside of me more than anything else had. It didn't make sense.

"I don't know, Marlene," I said. "I just do."

"Love is possible, Lisette. I know you're jaded and don't believe in it, but it is possible. Trust me, after all of the bullshit with Steve, I was prepared to swear off of it forever too, but just when I was ready to do that, Michael came into my life."

I groaned. I really didn't want to hear any of her sappy shit.

"Marlene . . ."

"I'm just saying, Lisette, what you do . . . the men you trap . . . not all of them are assholes. There are some decent ones out there. As much as you think there not, if you try to leave your door cracked open just a little bit, you'll see the right guy can come along and it could be a beautiful thing."

I clenched my jaw. Friend or not, I'd had enough. I said, "I don't do love, Marlene," and then I ended the call and turned my BlackBerry off. "Shit."

The bath water had grown tepid. I'd missed another replay of "Amado Mio."

I was irritated.

I turned the hot water faucet on, leaned my head back, closed my eyes, and put my focus back on the song that had no real relevance in my life. At least not in my current one.

"Amado Mio."

A song about being in love forever.

I breathed.

Listened to the song.

And as hard as I tried not to, I went back to a time I'd let go of a long time ago.